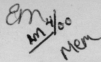

He sat back in his chair, watching her.

Presently he said, coldly polite, "Miss Beckworth, shall we begin as we intend to go on? I am aware that I am a poor substitute for Professor Smythe; nevertheless we have inherited each other whether we wish it or not. I must confess that you are not quite what I would have wished for, and I believe that you hold the same opinion of me. If you find it difficult to work for me, then by all means ask for a transfer. On the other hand, if you are prepared to put up with my lack of social graces, I daresay we may rub along quite nicely."

He smiled then, and she caught her breath, for he looked quite different—a man she would like to know.

Betty Neels spent her childhood and youth in Devonshire, England, before training as a nurse and midwife. She was an army nursing sister during the war, married a Dutchman, and subsequently lived in Holland for fourteen years. She now lives with her husband in Dorset, and has a daughter and grandson. Her hobbies are reading, animals, old buildings and writing. Betty started to write on retirement from nursing, incited by a lady in a library bemoaning the lack of romantic novels.

Books by Betty Neels

HARLEQUIN ROMANCE
3454—FATE TAKES A HAND
3467—THE RIGHT KIND OF GIRL
3483—THE MISTLETOE KISS
3492—MARRYING MARY

Don't miss any of our special offers. Write to us at the following address for information on our newest releases.

Harlequin Reader Service
U.S.: 3010 Walden Ave., P.O. Box 1325, Buffalo, NY 14269
Canadian: P.O. Box 609, Fort Erie, Ont. L2A 5X3

Betty Neels

A Kiss for Julie

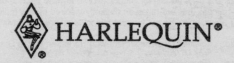

HARLEQUIN®

TORONTO • NEW YORK • LONDON
AMSTERDAM • PARIS • SYDNEY • HAMBURG
STOCKHOLM • ATHENS • TOKYO • MILAN • MADRID
PRAGUE • WARSAW • BUDAPEST • AUCKLAND

ISBN 0-373-03512-8

A KISS FOR JULIE

First North American Publication 1998.

CHAPTER ONE

PROFESSOR SMYTHE sat behind his cluttered desk, peering over his spectacles at the girl sitting on the other side of it. A very pretty girl, indeed he considered her beautiful, with bronze hair piled on top of her head, a charming nose, a gentle mouth and large green eyes fringed with bronze lashes.

She looked up from her notebook and smiled at him.

He took off his spectacles, polished them and put them back on again, ran his hand through the fringe of white hair encircling his bald patch and tugged his goatee beard. 'I've a surprise for you, Julie.' And at her sudden sharp glance he added, 'No, no, you're not being made redundant—I'm retiring at the end of the week. There, I meant to lead up to it gently—'

She said at once, 'You're ill—that must be the reason. No one would ever let you retire, sir.'

'Yes, I'm ill—not prostrate in bed, by any means, but I have to lead a quiet life, it seems, without delay.' He sighed. 'I shall miss this place and I shall miss you, Julie. How long is it since you started working for me?'

'Three years. I shall miss you too, Professor.'

'Do you want to know what is to happen to you?' he asked.

'Yes—yes, please, I do.'

5

'I am handing over to a Professor van der Driesma—a Dutchman widely acclaimed in our particular field of medicine. He works mostly at Leiden but he's been over here for some time, working at Birmingham and Edinburgh. What he doesn't know about haematology would barely cover a pin's head.' He smiled. 'I should know; he was my registrar at Edinburgh.' He went on, 'I'm handing you over to him, Julie; you'll be able to help him find his feet and make sure that he knows where to go and keep his appointments and so on. You've no objection?'

'No, sir. I'm truly sorry that you are retiring but I'll do my best to please Professor whatever-his-name-is.'

Professor Smythe sighed. 'Well, that's that. Now, what about Mrs Collins? Did you manage to get her old notes for me?'

Julie pushed a folder a little nearer to him. 'They go back a long way...'

'Yes, a most interesting case. I'll read them and then I shall want you to make a summary for me.' He tossed the papers on his desk around in front of him. 'Wasn't there a report I had to deal with?'

Julie got up, tall, splendidly built and unfussed. 'It's here, under your elbow, sir.' She fished the paper out for him and put it down under his nose.

He went away presently to see his patients and she settled down to her day's work. Secretary to someone as important as Professor Smythe was a job which didn't allow for slacking; her private worries about his leaving and the prospect of working for a stranger who might not approve of her had to be put aside until the evening.

Professor Smythe didn't refer to his departure again that day. She took the letters he dictated and went to her slip of a room adjoining his office, dealt with mislaid notes, answered the telephone and kept at bay anyone threatening to waste his precious time. A usual day, she reflected, wishing him goodnight at last and going out into the busy streets.

It was late September and the evening dusk cast a kindly veil over the dinginess of the rows of small houses and shabby shops encircling the hospital. Julie took a breath of unfresh air and went to queue for her bus.

St Bravo's was in Shoreditch, a large, ugly building with a long history and a splendid reputation, and since her home was close to Victoria Park the bus ride was fairly short.

She walked along the little street bordered by red-brick terraced houses, rounded the corner at its end, turned into a short drive leading to a solid Victorian house and went in through the back door. The kitchen was large and old-fashioned and there was an elderly man standing at the table, cutting bread and butter.

Julie took off her jacket. 'Hello, Luscombe. Lovely to be home; it seems to have been a long day.'

'Mondays always is, Miss Julie. Your ma's in the sitting room; I'll be along with the tea in two ticks.'

She took a slice of bread and butter as she went past him and crammed it into her pretty mouth. 'I'll come and help you with supper presently. Is it something nice? It was corned beef and those ready-made potatoes for lunch.'

'As nice a macaroni cheese as you'll find anywhere. I'll leave you to see to the pudding.'

She went out of the room, crossed the hall and
opened the door of a room on the other side of the
house. Mrs Beckworth was sitting at the table writing,
but she pushed the papers away as Julie went in.

'Hello, love. You're early; how nice. I'm dying for
a cup of tea...'

'Luscombe's bringing it.' Julie sat down near her
mother. 'I can't imagine life without him, can you,
Mother?'

'No, dear. I've been checking the bills. Do you
suppose we could afford to get Esme that hockey stick
she says she simply must have? Yours is a bit old, I
suppose.'

Julie thought. 'I had it for my fifteenth birthday;
that's almost twelve years ago. Let's afford it.'

Her mother said unexpectedly, 'You ought to be
enjoying yourself, Julie—finding a husband...'

'I'll wait until he finds me, Mother, dear. I'm very
happy at St Bravo's. Professor Smythe's a dear.' She
hesitated. 'He's leaving at the end of the week—he's
not well. I'm to be handed over to his successor—a
Dutchman with the kind of name you never
remember!'

'Do you mind?'

'I shall miss Professor Smythe—he's a dear old
man—but no, I don't mind.' She would have minded,
she reflected, if she had been told that her services
were no longer required; her salary was something that
they couldn't do without.

Luscombe came in with the tea then, and they talked
of other things—Michael, Julie's elder brother, a
houseman at a Birmingham hospital; David, still at
Cambridge, reading ancient history and intent on be-
coming a schoolmaster, and Esme, the baby of the

family, fourteen years old and a pupil at the local grammar school.

'Where is she, by the way?' asked Julie.

'Having tea at the Thompsons'. She promised to be back here by half past six. The Thompson boy will walk her round.'

Julie peered into the empty teapot. 'Well, I'll go and make a bread-and-butter pudding, shall I?'

'That would be nice, dear. Esme popped in on her way from school and took Blotto with her. The Thompsons don't mind.'

'Good. I'll give him a run in the park later on.'

Her mother frowned. 'I don't like you going out after dark.'

'I'll not be alone, dear; Blotto will be with me.' She smiled widely. 'Besides, I'm hardly what you would describe as a delicate female, am I?'

She was in the kitchen when Esme came home, bringing with her the Thompson boy, Freddie, and Blotto, a dog of assorted ancestry with a long, sweeping tail and a rough coat. He was a large dog and he looked fierce, but his disposition was that of a lamb. However, as Julie pointed out, what did that matter when he looked fierce?

Freddie didn't stay; he was a frequent visitor to the house and came and went casually. He bade Julie a polite goodbye, lifted a hand in farewell to Esme and took himself off, leaving the younger girl to feed Blotto and then, spurred on by Julie, to finish her homework. 'And we'll go on Saturday and get that hockey stick,' said Julie.

Esme flung herself at her. 'Julie, you darling. Really? The one I want? Not one of those horrid cheap ones.'

'The one you want, love.'

Getting ready for bed in her room later that evening, Julie allowed her thoughts to dwell on the future. She did this seldom, for as far as she could see there wasn't much point in doing so. She must learn to be content with her life.

No one had expected her father to die of a heart attack and they were lucky to have this house to live in. It was too large and needed a lot done to it, but it was cheaper to continue to live in it than to find something more modern and smaller. Besides, when she had made tentative enquiries of a house agent, he had told her that if they sold the place they would get a very poor price—barely enough to buy anything worth living in. It was a pity that there had been very little money, and what there had been had gone to get the boys started.

Julie sighed and picked up her hairbrush. It would be nice to get married—to meet a man who wouldn't mind shouldering the burden of a widowed mother, two brothers and a schoolgirl sister. Her sensible mind told her that she might as well wish for the moon.

She brushed her mane of hair and jumped into bed. She hoped that the professor who was taking her over would be as nice an old man as Professor Smythe. Perhaps, she thought sleepily, as he was Dutch, he would go back to Holland from time to time, leaving her to deal with things or be loaned out to other consultants as and when required. It would make a change.

*   *   *

There was a good deal of extra work to be done during the rest of the week; Professor Smythe tended to be forgetful and occasionally peevish when he mislaid something. Julie dealt with him patiently, used to his sudden little spurts of temper. Besides, she reasoned after a particularly trying morning, he wasn't well.

It was on the last morning—Friday—as she patiently waded through the filing cabinet for notes which Professor Smythe simply had to have when the door opened behind her and she turned to see who it was.

Any girl's dream, she thought, and, since he had ignored her and crossed to Professor Smythe's office, turned back to her files. But she had even in those few seconds taken a good look. Tall—six and a half feet, perhaps—and enormous with it, and pale hair— so pale that there might be grey hair too. His eyes, she felt sure, would be blue.

'Come here, Julie, and meet your new boss,' called Professor Smythe.

She entered his office, closed the door carefully and crossed the room, glad for once that she was a tall girl and wouldn't have to stretch her neck to look at him.

'Professor van der Driesma,' said Professor Smythe. 'Simon, this is Julie Beckworth; I'm sure you'll get on famously.'

She held out a polite hand and had it crushed briefly. She wasn't as sure as Professor Smythe about getting on famously, though. His eyes *were* blue; they were cold too, and indifferent. He wasn't going to like her. She sought frantically for the right thing to say and murmured, 'How do you do?' which didn't sound right somehow.

He didn't waste words but nodded at her and turned to Professor Smythe. 'I wonder if we might go over these notes—that patient in the women's ward—Mrs Collins—there are several problems...'

'Ah, yes, you are quite right, Simon. Now, as I see it...'

Julie went back to her filing cabinet, and when told to take her coffee-break went away thankfully. When she got back her new boss had gone.

He came again that afternoon when she was at her desk, dealing with the last of the paperwork before Professor Smythe handed over. The door separating her office from Professor Smythe's was open but when he came in he paused to close it—an action which caused her to sit up very straight and let out an explosive word. Did he imagine that she would eavesdrop? Professor Smythe had conducted countless interviews with the door wide open. A bad start, reflected Julie, thumping the computer with unnecessary force.

She would have been even more indignant if she could have heard what the two men were talking about.

'I should like to know more about Miss Beckworth,' observed Professor van der Driesma. 'I am indeed fortunate to have her, but if I were to know rather more of her background it might make for a speedier rapport between us.'

'Of course, Simon. I should have thought of that sooner. She has been with me for three years; I believe I told you that. Her father had a practice near Victoria Park, died suddenly of a massive heart attack—he was barely fifty-six years old. A splendid man, had a big practice, never expected to die young, of course, and left almost no money.

'Luckily the house was his; they still live in it— Julie, her mother and her young sister. There are two boys—the eldest's at the Birmingham General, his first post after qualifying, and the other boy's at Cambridge. I imagine they are poor, but Julie is hardly a young woman to talk about herself and I wouldn't presume to ask. She's a clever girl, very patient and hard-working, well liked too; you will find her a splendid right hand when you need one.' He chuckled. 'All this and beautiful besides.'

His companion smiled. 'How old is she? There is no question of her leaving to marry?'

'Twenty-six. Never heard of a boyfriend let alone a prospective husband. Even if she didn't tell me, the hospital grapevine would have got hold of it. Her home is nearby and she doesn't watch the clock and I've never known her to be late.'

'A paragon,' observed his companion drily.

'Indeed, yes. You are a lucky man, Simon.'

To which Professor van der Driesma made no reply. He glanced at his watch. 'I'm due on the wards; I'd better go. I shall hope to see something of you when you have retired, sir.'

'Of course, Mary and I will be delighted to see you at any time. I shall be interested to know how you get on. I'm sure you'll like the post.'

'I'm looking forward to it. I'll see you tomorrow before you leave.'

He went away, adding insult to injury by leaving the door open on his way out.

* * *

Professor Smythe had refused an official leave-taking but his friends and colleagues poured into his office on Saturday morning. Julie, who didn't work on a Saturday, was there, keeping in the background as well as her splendid shape allowed, making coffee, finding chairs and answering the phone, which rang incessantly. Presently the last of the visitors went away and Professor Smythe was left with just his successor and Julie.

'I'm off,' he told them. 'Thank you, Julie, for coming in to give a hand.' He trotted over to her and kissed her cheek. 'My right hand; I shall miss you. You must come and see us.'

She shook his hand and saw how tired he looked. 'Oh, I will, please.' She proffered a small book. 'I hope you'll like this—a kind of memento...'

It was a small book on birds and probably he had it already, for he was a keen bird-watcher, but he received it with delight, kissed her again and said, 'Be off with you, Julie.'

He would want to talk to Professor van der Driesma she thought, and went silently, closing the door behind her. She was crossing the forecourt when a dark grey Bentley crept up beside her and stopped. Professor van der Driesma got out.

He said without preamble, 'I'll drive you home.'

'My bus goes from across the street. Thank you for the offer, though.' She was coolly polite, remembering the closed door. Rude man...

'Get in.' Nicely said, but he wasn't prepared to argue. After all, she was working for him from now on. She got in.

He got in beside her. 'Somewhere on the other side of Victoria Park, isn't it? Professor Smythe told me that your father was a GP.'

'Yes.' She added baldly, 'He died.'

'I'm sorry,' he said, and strangely enough she knew that he meant it.

'I think that I should warn you that I may work at a slightly faster pace than Professor Smythe.'

'That's to be expected,' said Julie crisply. 'He's very elderly and ill too, and you're . . .' she paused. 'You're not quite middle-aged, are you?'

'Not quite. If I work you too hard you must tell me, Miss Beckworth.'

Put neatly in her place, she said, 'You can turn left here and then right. It's a short cut.'

If he was surprised to see the roomy house with its rather untidy garden, surrounded by narrow streets of small dwellings, he said nothing. He drew up in the road and got out to open her door—an action which impressed her, even if against her will. He might have a nasty tongue but his manners were perfect and effortless.

'Thank you, Professor,' she said politely, not to be outdone. 'I'll be at the office at eight forty-five on Monday morning.'

He closed the gate behind her, aware of faces peering from several windows in the house, waited until she had reached the door and opened it and then got into his car and drove away. He smiled as he drove.

Julie was met in the hall by her mother, Esme and Luscombe.

'Whoever was that?' her mother wanted to know.

'That's a smashing car,' observed Luscombe.

'He's a giant,' said Esme.

'That's my new boss. He gave me a lift home. His name is Simon van der Driesma; I don't think he likes me . . .'

'Why ever not?' Her mother was simply astonished; everyone liked Julie. 'Why did he give you a lift, then?'

'I think he may have wanted to see where I lived.'

Mrs Beckworth, who had hoped that there might be other reasons—after all, Julie was a beautiful girl and excellent company—said in a disappointed voice, 'Oh, well, perhaps. We waited lunch for you, love. One of Luscombe's splendid casseroles.'

Luscombe, besides having been with them for as long as Julie could remember, first as a general factotum in her father's surgery and then somehow taking over the housekeeping, was a splendid cook. 'I'm ravenous,' said Julie.

They went to the sports shop after lunch and bought Esme's hockey stick, and Esme went round to the Thompsons' later to show it off to Freddie while Julie took Blotto for his evening walk.

Sunday, as all Sundays, went too quickly—church, home to an economical pot-roast, and then a few lazy hours reading the Sunday papers until it was time to get the tea.

Luscombe went to see his married sister on Sunday afternoons, so Julie got their supper, loaded the washing machine ready to switch it on in the morning, did some ironing, made sure that Esme had everything ready for school, had a cosy chat with her mother and took herself off to bed. She went to sleep quickly, but only after a few anxious thoughts about the next morning. Even if Professor van der Driesma didn't like her overmuch, as long as she did as he wished and remembered to hold her tongue it might not be so bad.

It was a bad start on Monday morning. She was punctual as always, but he was already there, sitting at his desk, his reading glasses perched on his patrician nose, perusing some papers lying before him then laying them tidily aside.

'Good morning, sir,' said Julie, and waited.

He glanced up. His 'good morning' was grave; she hoped that he would soon get out of the habit of calling her Miss Beckworth; it made her feel old.

'I believe I am to do a ward round at ten o'clock. Perhaps you will get the patients' notes and bring them to me here.' When she hesitated, he said, 'Yes, I am aware that the ward sister should have them, but I simply wish to glance through them before I do my round.'

Julie went up to the women's medical ward and found Sister in her office. Sister was small and dainty, never lacking dates with the more senior housemen. She was drinking strong tea from a battered mug and waved Julie to the only chair. 'Have some tea—I'll get one of the nurses—'

'I'd love a cup, but I don't dare,' said Julie. 'Professor van der Driesma wants the notes of his patients on the ward so's he can study them before his round.'

'A bit different to Professor Smythe?' asked Sister, hunting up folders on her desk. 'I must say he's remarkably good-looking; my nurses are drooling over him but I don't think he's even noticed them. A bit reserved?'

'I don't know, but I think you may be right.' She took the bundle of notes. 'I'll get these back to you as soon as I can, Sister.'

'I'll have your head if you don't,' said Sister. 'It's his first round and it has to be perfect.'

Julie skimmed back through the hospital, laid the folders on the professor's desk and waited.

He said thank you without looking up and she slid away to her own desk to type up notes and reports and answer the telephone. Just before ten o'clock, however, she went back to his desk.

'Shall I take the patients' notes back now, sir?' she asked the bowed head; his glasses were on the end of his nose and he was making pencil notes in the margin of the report that he was reading.

He glanced up and spoke mildly. 'Is there any need? I can take them with me.' When she hesitated he said, 'Well?'

'Sister Griffiths wanted them back before you went on the ward.'

He gave her a brief look and said, 'Indeed? Then we mustn't disappoint her, must we? Oh, and you may as well stay on the ward and take notes.'

She gathered up the folders. 'Very well, sir. Do you want me to come back here for you? It is almost ten o'clock.'

'No, no, save your feet!'

It was a remark which made her feel as if she had bunions or painful corns. It rankled, for she had excellent feet, narrow and high-arched, and while she spent little money on her clothes she bought good shoes. Plain court shoes with not too high heels, kept beautifully polished.

From his desk the professor watched her go, aware that he had annoyed her and irritated by it. He hoped that her prickly manner would soften, totally unaware that it was he who was making it prickly. He didn't waste time thinking about her; he put the notes he had been making in his pocket and took himself off to Women's Medical.

He had a number of patients there; a rare case of aplastic anaemia—the only treatment of which was frequent blood transfusions, two young women with leukaemia, an older woman with Hodgkin's disease and two cases of polycythaemia. To each he gave his full attention, taking twice as long as Sister had expected, dictating to Julie as he went in a quiet, unhurried voice.

She, wrestling with long words like agranulocytosis and lymphosarcoma, could see that the patients liked him. So did Sister, her annoyance at the length of the round giving way to her obvious pleasure in his company. It was a pity that he didn't appear to show any pleasure in hers; his attention was focused on his patients; he had few words to say to her and those he had were of a purely professional kind.

As for Julie, he dictated to her at length, over one shoulder, never once looking to see if she knew what he was talking about. Luckily, she did; Professor Smythe had been a good deal slower but the words he had used had been just as long. She had taken care over the years to have a medical directory handy when she was typing up notes, although from time to time she had asked him to explain a word or a medical term to her and he had done so readily.

She thought that it would be unlikely for Professor van der Driesma to do that. Nor would he invite her to share his coffee-break while he told her about his grandchildren... He was too young for grandchildren, of course, but probably he had children. Pretty little girls, handsome little boys, a beautiful wife.

She became aware that he had stopped speaking and looked up. He was staring at her so coldly that she had a moment's fright that she had missed something he had said. If she had, she would get it from Sister later. She shut her notebook with a snap and he said, 'I'd like those notes as soon as you can get them typed, Miss Beckworth.'

'Very well, sir,' said Julie, and promised herself silently that she would have her coffee first.

Which she did, prudently not spending too much time doing so; somehow the professor struck her as a man not given to wasting time in Sister's office chatting over coffee and a tin of biscuits. She was right; she was halfway through the first batch of notes when he returned.

'I shall be in the path lab if I'm wanted,' he told her, and went away again.

Julie applied herself to her work. It was all going to be quite different, she thought regretfully; life would never be the same again.

The professor stayed away for a long time; she finished her notes, placed them on his desk and took herself off to the canteen for her midday meal. She shared her table with two other secretaries and one of the receptionists, all of them agog to know about the new professor.

'What's he like?' asked the receptionist, young and pretty and aware of it.

'Well, I don't really know, do I?' said Julie reasonably. 'I mean, I've only seen him for a few minutes this morning and on the ward round.' She added cautiously, 'He seems very nice.'

'You'll miss Professor Smythe,' said one of the secretaries, middle-aged and placid. 'He was an old dear...'

The receptionist laughed, 'Well, this one certainly isn't that. He's got more than his fair share of good looks too. Hope he comes to my desk one day!'

Julie thought that unlikely, but she didn't say so. She ate her cold meat, potatoes, lettuce leaf and half a tomato, followed this wholesome but dull fare with prunes and custard and went back to her little office. She would make herself tea; Professor Smythe had installed an electric kettle and she kept a teapot and mugs in the bottom drawer of one of the filing cabinets—sugar too, and tiny plastic pots of milk.

Professor van der Driesma was sitting at his desk. He looked up as she went in. 'You have been to your lunch?' he asked smoothly. 'Perhaps you would let me know when you will be absent from the office.'

Julie glowered; never mind if he was a highly important member of the medical profession, there was such a thing as pleasant manners between colleagues. 'If you had been here to tell, I would have told you,' she pointed out in a chilly voice. 'And it's not lunch, it's midday dinner.'

He sat back in his chair, watching her. Presently he said, coldly polite, 'Miss Beckworth, shall we begin as we intend to go on? I am aware that I am a poor substitute for Professor Smythe; nevertheless, we have inherited each other whether we wish it or not. Shall we endeavour to make the best of things?

'I must confess that you are not quite what I would have wished for and I believe that you hold the same opinion of me. If you find it difficult to work for me, then by all means ask for a transfer. Your work is highly regarded; there should be no difficulty in that. On the other hand, if you are prepared to put up with my lack of the social graces, I dare say we may rub along quite nicely.'

He smiled then, and she caught her breath, for he looked quite different—a man she would like to know, to be friends with. She said steadily, 'I would prefer to stay if you will allow that. You see, you're not a bit like Professor Smythe, but I'm sure once I've got used to you you'll find me satisfactory.' She added, 'What don't you like about me?'

'Did I say that I disliked you? Indeed I did not; I meant that you were not quite the secretary I would have employed had I been given the choice.'

'Why?'

'You're too young—and several other...' He paused. 'Shall we let it rest?' He stood up and held out a hand. 'Shall we shake on it?'

She shook hands and thought what a strange conversation they were having.

He was back behind his desk, turning over the papers before him.

'This case of agranulocytosis—Mrs Briggs has had typhoid and has been treated with chloramphenicol, the cause of her condition. I should like to see any old notes if she has been a patient previously. From her present notes you have seen that she remembers being here on two occasions but she can't remember when. Is that a hopeless task?'

'Probably. I'll let you have them as soon as possible. The path lab from the Royal Central phoned; they would like to speak to you when you are free.'

'Ah, yes. There's a patient there. Get hold of them and put them through to me, will you, Miss Beckworth?'

'I'm going to hunt for those notes,' she told him. 'I shall be in the records office until I find them.'

'Very well.' He didn't look up from his writing and she went to her own office, dialled the Royal Central and presently put the call through to his office. There was nothing on her desk that needed urgent attention, so she went through the hospital and down into the basement and, after a few words with the fussy woman in charge of the patients' records, set to work.

It was a difficult task but not entirely hopeless. Mrs Briggs was forty years old; her recollections of her previous visits were vague but positive. Say, anything between five and ten years ago... It was tiresome work and dusty and the fussy woman or her assistant should have given her a hand, although in all fairness she had to admit that they were being kept busy enough.

She longed for a cup of tea, and a glance at her watch told her that her teabreak was long past. Was she supposed to stay until the notes were found or could she go home at half-past five? she wondered.

It was almost five o'clock when her luck turned and, looking rather less than her pristine self, she went back to the professor's office.

He was on the telephone as she went in; she laid the folders down on his desk and, since he nodded without looking up, she went to her office and sat down at her own desk. While she had been away someone had tossed a variety of paperwork onto it.

'No tea,' muttered Julie, 'and this lot to polish off before I go home, and much thanks shall I get for it—'

'Ah, no, Miss Beckworth,' said the professor from somewhere behind her. 'Do not be so hard on me. You have found the notes, for which I thank you, and a dusty job it was too from the look of you.'

She turned round indignantly at that and he went on smoothly, 'A pot of tea would help, wouldn't it? And most of the stuff on your desk can wait until the morning.'

He leaned across her and picked up the phone. 'The canteen number?' he asked her, and when she gave it ordered with pleasant courtesy, and with a certainty that no one would object, a tray of tea for two and a plate of buttered toast.

She was very conscious of the vast size of him. She wondered, idiotically, if he had played rugger in his youth. Well, she conceded, he wasn't all that old—thirty-five, at the most forty... He had straightened up, towering over her, his gaze intent, almost as though he had read her thoughts and was amused by them. She looked at the clock and said in a brisk voice, 'I can get a good deal of this done this afternoon, sir. I'm quite willing to stay on for a while.'

'I said that tomorrow morning would do.' His voice was mild but dared her to argue. 'We will have our tea and you will leave at your usual time.'

She said 'Very well, sir' in a meek voice, although she didn't feel meek. Who did he think he was? Professor or no professor, she had no wish to be ordered about.

'You'll get used to me in time,' he observed, just as though she had voiced the thought out loud. 'Here is the tea.'

The canteen server put the tray down on his desk; none of the canteen staff was particularly friendly with those who took their meals there; indeed, at times one wondered if they grudged handing over the plates of food, and the girl who had come in was not one of Julie's favourites—handing out, as she did, ill nature with meat and two veg. Now, miraculously, she was actually smiling. Not at Julie, of course, and when he thanked her politely she muttered, 'No trouble, sir; any time. I can always pop along with something.'

The professor sat down behind his desk. 'Come and pour out,' he suggested, 'and let us mull over tomorrow's schedule.' He handed her the toast and bit hugely into his. 'What an obliging girl.'

'Huh,' said Julie. 'She practically throws our dinners at us. But then, of course, you're a man.'

'Er—yes; presumably you think that makes a difference?'

'Of course it does.' Perhaps she wasn't being quite polite; she added 'sir'.

They had little to say to each other; indeed, he made a couple of phone calls while he polished off the toast, and when they had had second cups he said, 'Off you go, Miss Beckworth; I'll see you in the morning.'

CHAPTER TWO

WHEN Julie got home they were all waiting to hear how she had got on.

'At least he didn't keep you late,' observed her mother. 'Is he nice?' By which she meant was he good-looking, young and liable to fall in love with Julie?

'Abrupt, immersed in his work, likes things done at once, very nice with his patients—'

'Old?' Mrs Beckworth tried hard to sound casual.

'Getting on for forty, perhaps thirty-five; it's hard to tell.' Julie took pity on her mother. 'He's very good-looking, very large, and I imagine the nurses are all agog.'

'Not married?' asked her mother hopefully.

'I don't know, Mother, and I doubt if I ever shall; he's not chatty.'

'Sounds OK to me,' said Luscombe, 'even if he's foreign.'

Esme had joined the inquisition. 'He's Dutch; does he talk with a funny accent?'

'No accent at all—well, yes, perhaps you can hear that he's not English, but only because he speaks it so well, if you see what I mean.'

'A gent?' said Luscombe.

'Well, yes, and frightfully clever, I believe. I dare say that once we've got used to each other we shall get on very well.'

'What do you call him?' asked Esme.

'Professor or sir...'

'What does he call you?'

'Miss Beckworth.'

Esme hooted with laughter. 'Julie, that makes you sound like an elderly spinster. I bet he wears glasses...'

'As a matter of fact he does—for reading.'

'He sounds pretty stuffy,' said Esme. 'Can we have tea now that Julie's home?'

'On the table in two ticks,' said Luscombe, and went back to the kitchen to fetch the macaroni cheese—for tea for the Beckworths was that unfashionable meal, high tea—a mixture of supper and tea taken at the hour of half past six, starting with a cooked dish, going on to bread and butter and cheese or sandwiches, jam and scones, and accompanied by a large pot of tea.

Only on Sundays did they have afternoon tea, and supper at a later hour. And if there were guests— friends or members of the family—then a splendid dinner was conjured up by Luscombe; the silver was polished, the glasses sparkled and a splendid damask cloth that Mrs Beckworth cherished was brought out. They might be poor but no one needed to know that.

Now they sat around the table, enjoying Luscombe's good food, gossiping cheerfully, and if they still missed the scholarly man who had died so suddenly they kept that hidden. Sometimes, Julie reflected, three years seemed a long time, but her father was as clear in her mind as if he were living, and she knew that her mother and Esme felt the same. She had no doubt that the faithful Luscombe felt the same way, too.

She had hoped that after the professor's offer of tea and toast he would show a more friendly face, but she was to be disappointed. His 'Good morning, Miss Beckworth' returned her, figuratively speaking, to arm's length once more. Of course, after Professor Smythe's avuncular 'Hello, Julie' it was strange to be addressed as Miss Beckworth. Almost everyone in the hospital called her Julie; she hoped that he might realise that and follow suit.

He worked her hard, but since he worked just as hard, if not harder, himself she had no cause for complaint. Several days passed in uneasy politeness—cold on his part, puzzled on hers. She would get used to him, she told herself one afternoon, taking his rapid dictation, and glanced up to find him staring at her. 'Rather as though I was something dangerous and ready to explode,' she explained to her mother later.

'Probably deep in thought and miles away,' said Mrs Beckworth, and Julie had to agree.

There was no more tea and toast; he sent her home punctiliously at half past five each day and she supposed that he worked late at his desk clearing up the paperwork, for much of his day was spent on the wards or in consultation. He had a private practice too, and since he was absent during the early afternoons she supposed that he saw those patients then. A busy day, but hers was busy too.

Of course, she was cross-examined about him each time she went to the canteen, but she had nothing to tell—and even if she had had she was discreet and loyal and would not have told. Let the man keep his private life to himself, she thought.

Professor van der Driesma, half-aware of the interest in him at St Bravo's, ignored it. He was a haematologist first and last, and other interests paled beside his deep interest in his work and his patients.

He did have other interests, of course: a charming little mews cottage behind a quiet, tree-lined street and another cottage near Henley, its little back garden running down to the river, and, in Holland, other homes and his family home.

He had friends too, any number of them, as well as his own family. His life was full and he had pushed the idea of marriage aside for the time being. No one—no woman—had stirred his heart since he had fallen in love as a very young man to be rejected for an older one, already wealthy and high in his profession. He had got over the love years ago—indeed he couldn't imagine now what he had seen in the girl—but her rejection had sown the seeds of a determination to excel at his work.

Now he had fulfilled that ambition, but in the meantime he had grown wary of the pretty girls whom his friends were forever introducing him to; he wanted more than a pretty girl—he wanted an intelligent companion, someone who knew how to run his home, someone who would fit in with his friends, know how to entertain them, would remove from him the petty burden of social life. She would need to be good-looking and elegant and dress well too, and bring up their children...

He paused there. There was no such woman, of course; he wanted perfection and there was, he decided cynically, no such thing in a woman; he would eventually have to make the best of it with the nearest to his ideal.

These thoughts, naturally enough, he kept to himself; no one meeting him at a dinner party or small social gathering would have guessed that behind his bland, handsome face he was hoping that he might meet the woman he wanted to marry. In the meantime there was always his work.

Which meant that there was work for Julie too; he kept her beautiful nose to the grindstone, but never thoughtlessly; she went home punctually each evening—something she had seldom done with Professor Smythe. He also saw to it that she had her coffee-break, her midday dinner and her cup of tea at three o'clock, but between these respites he worked her hard.

She didn't mind; indeed, she found it very much to her taste as, unlike his predecessor, he was a man of excellent memory, as tidy as any medical man was ever likely to be, and not given to idle talk. It would be nice, she reflected, watching his enormous back going through the door, if he dropped the occasional word other than some diabolical medical term that she couldn't spell. Still, they got on tolerably well, she supposed. Perhaps at a suitable occasion she might suggest that he stopped calling her Miss Beckworth... At Christmas, perhaps, when the entire hospital was swamped with the Christmas spirit.

It was during their second week of uneasy association that he told her that he would be going to Holland at the weekend. She wasn't surprised at that, for he had international renown, but she was surprised to find a quick flash of regret that he was going away; she supposed that she had got used to the silent figure at his desk or his disappearing for hours on end to return wanting something impossible at the drop of a hat. She said inanely, 'How nice—nice for you, sir.'

'I shall be working,' he told her austerely. 'And do not suppose that you will have time to do more than work either.'

'Why do you say that, Professor? Do you intend leaving me a desk piled high?' Her delightful bosom swelled with annoyance. 'I can assure you that I shall have plenty to do...'

'You misunderstand me, Miss Beckworth; you will be going with me. I have a series of lectures to give and I have been asked to visit two hospitals and attend a seminar. You will take any notes I require and type them up.'

She goggled at him. 'Will I?' She added coldly, 'And am I to arrange for our travel and where we are to stay and transport?'

He sat back at ease. 'No, no. That will all be attended to; all you will need will be a portable computer and your notebook and pencil. You will be collected from your home at nine o'clock on Saturday morning. I trust you will be ready at that time.'

'Oh, I'll be ready,' said Julie, and walked over to his desk to stand before it looking at him. 'It would have been nice to have been asked,' she observed with a snap. 'I do have a life beyond these walls, you know.'

With which telling words she walked into her own office and shut the door. There was a pile of work on her desk; she ignored it. She had been silly to lose her temper; it might cost her her job. But she wasn't going to apologise.

'I will not be ordered about; I wouldn't talk to Blotto in such a manner.' She had spoken out loud and the professor's answer took her by surprise.

'My dear Miss Beckworth, I have hurt your feelings. I do apologise; I had no intention of ruffling your temper.' A speech which did nothing to improve matters.

'That's all right,' said Julie, still coldly.

She was formulating a nasty remark about slave-drivers when he asked, 'Who or what is Blotto? Who, I presume, is treated with more courtesy than I show you.'

He had come round her desk and was sitting on its edge, upsetting the papers there. He was smiling at her too. She had great difficulty in not smiling back. 'Blotto is the family dog,' she told him, and looked away.

Professor van der Driesma was a kind man but he had so immersed himself in his work that he also wore an armour of indifference nicely mitigated by good manners. Now he set himself to restore Julie's good humour.

'I dare say that you travelled with Professor Smythe from time to time, so you will know what to take with you and the normal routine of such journeys...'

'I have been to Bristol, Birmingham and Edinburgh with Professor Smythe,' said Julie, still icily polite.

'Amsterdam, Leiden and Groningen, where we shall be going, are really not much farther away from London. I have to cram a good deal of work into four or five days; I must depend upon your support, which I find quite admirable.'

'I don't need to be buttered up,' said Julie, her temper as fiery as her hair. 'It's my job.'

'My dear Miss Beckworth, I shall forget that remark. I merely give praise where praise is due.' His voice was mild and he hid a smile. Julie really was a lovely girl but as prickly as a thorn-bush. Highly efficient too—everything that Professor Smythe had said of her; to have her ask for a transfer and leave him at the mercy of some chit of a girl... The idea was unthinkable. He observed casually, 'I shall, of course, be occupied for most of my days, but there will be time for you to do some sightseeing.'

It was tempting bait; a few days in another country, being a foreigner in another land—even with the professor for company it would be a nice change. Besides, she reminded herself, she had no choice; she worked for him and was expected to do as she was bid. She had, she supposed, behaved badly. She looked up at him. 'Of course I'll be ready to go with you, sir. I'm—I'm sorry I was a little taken aback; it was unexpected.'

He got off the desk. 'I am at times very forgetful,' he told her gravely. 'You had better bring a raincoat and an umbrella with you; it will probably rain. Let me have those notes as soon as possible, will you? I shall be up on the ward if I'm wanted.'

She would have to work like a maniac if she was to finish by half past five, she thought, but Julie sat for a few minutes, her head filled with the important problem of what clothes to take with her. Would she go out at all socially? She had few clothes, although those she had were elegant and timeless in style; blouses, she thought, the skirt she had on, the corduroy jacket that she'd bought only a few weeks ago, just in case it was needed, a dress... Her eyes lighted on the clock and she left her pleasant thoughts for some hard work.

She told her mother as soon as she got home and within minutes Esme and Luscombe had joined them to hear the news.

'Clothes?' said Mrs Beckworth at once. 'You ought to have one of those severe suits with padded shoulders; the women on TV wear them all the time; they look like businessmen.'

'I'm not a businessman, Mother, dear! And I'd hate to wear one. I've got that dark brown corduroy jacket and this skirt—a pleated green and brown check. I'll take a dress and a blouse for each day...'

'Take that smoky blue dress—the one you've had for years,' said Esme at once. 'It's so old it's fashionable again. Will you go out a lot—restaurants and dancing? Perhaps he'll take you to a nightclub.'

'The professor? I should imagine that wild horses wouldn't drag him into one. And of course he won't take me out. I'll have piles of work to do and he says he will be fully occupied each day.'

'You might meet a man,' observed Esme. 'You know—and he'll be keen on you and take you out in the evenings. The professor can't expect you to work all the time.'

'I rather fancy that's just what he does expect. But it'll be fun and I'll bring you all back something really Dutch. Blotto too.'

She had two days in which to get herself ready, which meant that each evening she was kept busy—washing her abundant hair, doing her nails, pressing the blouses, packing a case.

'Put in a woolly,' suggested her mother, peering over her shoulder. 'Two—that nice leaf-brown cardigan you had for Christmas last year and the green sweater.' She frowned. 'You're sure we can't afford one of those suits?'

'Positive. I'll do very well with what I've got, and if Professor van der Driesma doesn't approve that's just too bad. Anyway, he won't notice.'

In this she was mistaken; his polite, uninterested glance as she opened the door to him on Saturday morning took in every small detail. He had to concede that although she looked businesslike she also looked feminine; with a lovely face such as hers she should be able to find herself an eligible husband...

He gave her a 'good morning,' unsmiling, was charming to her mother when he was introduced, and smiled at Esme's eager, 'You'll give Julie time to send some postcards, won't you?' He picked up Julie's case and was brought to a halt by Esme. 'Don't you get tired of seeing all that blood? Isn't it very messy?'

Mrs Beckworth's shocked 'Esme' was ignored.

'Well, I'm only asking,' said Esme.

The professor put the case down. 'There is almost no blood,' he said apologetically. 'Just small samples in small tubes and, more importantly, the condition of the patient—whether they're pale or yellow or red in the face. How ill they feel, how they look.'

Esme nodded. 'I'm glad you explained. I'm going to be a doctor.'

'I have no doubt you'll do very well.' He smiled his sudden charming smile. 'We have to go, I'm afraid.'

Julie bent to say goodbye to Blotto, kissed her mother and sister, and kissed Luscombe on his leathery cheek. 'Take care of them, Luscombe.'

'Leave 'em to me, Miss Julie; 'ave a good time.'

She got into the car; they were all so sure that she was going to enjoy herself but she had her doubts.

The professor had nothing to say for some time; he crossed the river and sped down the motorway towards Dover. 'You are comfortable?' he wanted to know.

'Yes, thank you. I don't think one could be anything else in a car like this.'

It was an observation which elicited no response from him. Was she going to spend four or five days in the company of a man who only addressed her when necessary? He addressed her now. 'You're very silent, Miss Beckworth.'

She drew a steadying breath; all the same there was peevishness in her voice. 'If you wished me to make conversation, Professor, I would have done my best.'

He laughed. 'I don't think I have ever met anyone quite like you. You fly—how do you say it?—off the handle without notice. At least it adds interest to life. I like your young sister.'

'Everyone likes her; she's such a dear girl and she says what she thinks...'

'It must run in the family!' Before she could utter he went on, 'She must miss her father.'

'Yes, we all do. He was a very special person...'

'You prefer not to talk about him?' His voice was kind.

'No. No, we talk about him a lot at home, but of course other people forget, or don't like to mention his name in case we get upset.'

'So—tell me something of him. Professor Smythe told me that he had a very large practice and his patients loved him.'

'Oh, they did, and he loved his work...' It was like a cork coming out of a bottle; she was in full flood, lost in happy reminiscences, and when she paused for breath the professor slipped in a quiet word or question and started her off again.

She was surprised to see that they were slowing as the outskirts of Dover slipped past them. 'I talk too much.'

'No, indeed not, Miss Beckworth; I have found it most interesting to know more of your father. You have a knack of holding one's interest.'

She muttered a reply, wondering if he was being polite, and they didn't speak much until he had driven the car on board the hovercraft and settled her in a seat. He took the seat beside her, ordered coffee and sandwiches, and with a word of excuse opened his briefcase and took out some papers.

The coffee was excellent and she was hungry. When she had finished she said, 'I'm going to tidy myself,' in an unselfconscious manner.

He matched it with a casual, 'Yes, do that; once we land I don't want to stop more than I have to.'

He got up to let her pass and, squeezing past him, she reflected that it was like circumnavigating a large and very solid tree-trunk.

Back in her seat once more, she looked out of the window and wondered how long it would take to drive to Leiden, which was to be their first stop.

Shortly afterwards they landed. 'We'll stop for a sandwich presently,' the professor assured her, stuffed her into the car and got in and drove off.

'Bruges, Antwerp, cross into Holland at Breda and drive on to the Hague; Leiden is just beyond.'

That, apparently, was as much as he intended to tell her. They were out of France and into Belgium before she saw the map in the pocket on the door. They were on a motorway, and such towns as they passed they skirted, but presently she started looking at signposts and traced their journey on the map. The

professor was driving fast but, she had to admit, with
a casual assurance which made her feel quite safe,
although it prevented her from seeing anything much.
But when they reached Bruges he slowed down and
said, to surprise her, 'This is a charming town; we'll
drive through it so that you get an idea of its beauty.'

Which he did, obligingly pointing out anything of
interest before rejoining the motorway once more. The
traffic was heavy here and Antwerp, as they ap-
proached it, loomed across the horizon. Before they
reached the city he turned off onto a ring road and
rejoined the motorway to the north of the city. Obviously, she thought, he knew the way—well, of course
he would since he went to and fro fairly frequently.
A huge road sign informed her that they were forty-
eight kilometres from Breda, and after some mental
arithmetic she decided on thirty miles. At the rate they
were going they would be there in less than half an
hour.

Which they were, still on the motorway skirting the
town, driving on towards the Moerdijk Bridge and
then on towards Rotterdam. Before they reached the
bridge the professor stopped by a roadside café,
parked the car and ushered her inside. It was a small
place, its tables half-filled. 'I'll be at that table by the
window,' he told her; he nodded to a door beside the
bar. 'Through there, don't be long—I'm hungry and
I expect you are too.'

She was famished, breakfast had been a meal taken
in another world, tea and dinner were as yet uncertain. She was back within five minutes.

'I've ordered for us both; I hope you'll enjoy my
choice. I'm having coffee but they'll bring you tea—
not quite as the English drink it, but at least it's tea.'

'Thank you, I'd love a cup. Are you making good time?'

'Yes. I hope to be at Leiden around teatime. You have a room close to the hospital. I shall want you tomorrow in the afternoon. In the morning I have several people to see so you will have time to look around. You may find the morning service at St Pieterskerk; it's a magnificent building.'

'I don't speak Dutch or understand it.'

'You don't need to—the service is similar to your own church, and if you need to ask the way practically everyone will understand you.'

'Then I'd like that.' The café owner had brought the coffee and, for her, a glass of hot water on a saucer with a teabag; he came back a moment later with two dishes on which reposed slices of bread covered with slices of ham and two fried eggs.

'This is an *uitsmijter*,' said the professor. 'If you don't care for it, say so, and I'll order something else.'

'It looks delicious.' She fell to; it not only looked good, it tasted good too, and, moreover, filled her empty insides up nicely. They ate without much talk; the professor was pleasant, thoughtful of her needs but not disposed to make idle conversation. Reasonable enough, she reflected, polishing off the last bits of ham; she had been wished on him and he didn't like her, although he concealed his dislike beneath good manners. At least he hadn't been able to fault her work...

They were back in the car within half an hour, heading towards Dordrecht and Rotterdam. As they left Dordrecht behind them the traffic became thicker, and as the outskirts of Rotterdam closed in on them she wondered how anyone ever found their way in the

tangle of traffic, but it appeared to hold no terrors
for her companion and presently they joined the long
line of cars edging through the Maas Tunnel and then
crossed the city and onto the motorway to den Haag.
It bypassed the city, but here and there there were
fields and copses which became more frequent as they
reached the outskirts of Leiden.

As Professor van der Driesma drove through its
heart Julie tried to see everything—it looked charming
with its lovely old houses and bustling streets—but
presently he turned into a wide street with a canal
running through its centre. 'Rapenburg,' the professor told her. 'The university and medical school
are on the right.'

Julie, outwardly calm, felt nervous. 'Will you be
there?' she asked.

'No, I shall be at my house.'

She waited for more but it seemed that that was all
she was to know. She persevered. 'Do you live here?'

'From time to time.' He wasn't going to say any
more and presently he stopped before a narrow, tall
house—one of a row of gabled houses just past the
university buildings. 'I think you will be comfortable
here.'

He got out, opened her door, got her case from the
boot and thumped the knocker on the solid front door.
The woman who opened it was tall and thin and
dressed severely in black, but she had a pleasant face
and kind smile.

The professor addressed her in Dutch before turning
to Julie. 'This is Mevrouw Schatt. She will show you
your room and give you your supper presently.'

He spoke to Mevrouw Schatt again, this time in
English. 'This is Miss Julie Beckworth, *mevrouw*. I

know you'll take care of her.' He turned back to Julie.
'I will call for you here at one o'clock tomorrow. Bring
your notebook with you. I'll tell you what I want you
to do when we are there.'

'Where?'

He looked surprised. 'Did I not tell you? We shall
be at the *aula* of the medical school—a discussion on
various types of anaemia. Mostly questions and
answers in English.'

Her 'very well, sir' sounded so meek that he gave
her a suspicious look, which she returned with a limpid
look from her green eyes.

He stood looking at her for a moment and she
thought that he was going to say something else, but
his 'Good evening, Miss Beckworth' was brisk. He
shook Mevrouw Schatt's hand and exchanged a
friendly remark. At least, Julie supposed that it was
friendly; she couldn't understand a word.

'Come, miss,' said Mevrouw Schatt, and led the
way up a steep flight of stairs and into a pleasant room
overlooking the canal. It was rather full of furniture
and the bed took up a great deal of space, but it was
spotless and warm.

They smiled at each other and Mevrouw Schatt said,
'The bathroom, along this passage. If you want anything you ask, miss.' She turned to go. 'I make tea
for you, if you will come down soon.'

Left alone, Julie tried the bed, looked out of the
window and unpacked what she would need for the
night. So far everything had gone smoothly. She only
hoped that she would be able to deal with the work.
Presently she went downstairs to sit in the living room
and have tea with her hostess.

The room was charming, the furniture old and gleaming, and there was a thick carpet underfoot, and heavy velvet curtains at the long windows which over-looked the street. Mevrouw Schatt switched on several little table-lamps so that the room was visible to passers-by. 'It is the custom,' she explained. 'We are pleased to let others see how cosily we live.'

While she drank her tea and ate the little biscuits Julie nodded and smiled and replied suitably, and wondered what the professor was doing. If he had liked her, surely she would have stayed at his house? Would his wife object? She presumed that he had one, for he had never evinced any interest in any of the staff at the hospital, and, if not a wife, a housekeeper...

Professor van der Driesma had gone straight to the hospital and checked with his colleagues that the ar-rangements for the following afternoon were satis-factory. It was a pity that the seminar had to be on a Sunday, but he had a tight schedule; he very much doubted if he would have time to go to his home, but at least he could spend the night at his home here in Leiden.

He drove there now, past the university again, over the canal and into a narrow street beside the imposing library. It was quiet here and the houses, narrow and four-storeyed, with their variety of gables, were to outward appearances exactly as they had been built three hundred years ago. He drove to the end and got out, mounted the double steps to the front door with its ornate transom and put his key into the modern lock to be greeted by a deep-throated barking, and as he opened the door a big, shaggy dog hurled himself at him.

The professor bore the onslaught with equanimity. 'Jason, old fellow; it's good to see you again.'

He turned to speak to the elderly, stout woman who had followed the dog into the narrow hall. 'Siska—nice to be home, even if only for one night.' He put an arm round her plump shoulders.

'I have an excellent tea ready,' she told him. 'It is a shame that you must dine out this evening.' She added wistfully, 'Perhaps you will soon spend more time here. You are so often in England.' She went on, 'If you would marry—find yourself a good little wife.'

'I'll think about it, Siska, if I can find one.'

He had his tea with Jason for company, and then the pair of them went for a long walk along the Rapenburg which led them past Mevrouw Schatt's house. He could see Julie sitting in the softly lighted room; she had Mevrouw Schatt's cat on her knee and was laughing.

He stopped to watch her for a moment. A beautiful girl, he reflected, and an excellent secretary; he had been agreeably surprised at her unflurried manner during their journey from England; with no fidgetting or demands to stop on the way, she had been an undemanding companion who didn't expect to be entertained. He walked on, forgetting her as soon as he started to mull over the next day's activities.

He was dining with friends that evening. He had known Gijs van der Eekerk since their student days together. Gijs had married young—a pretty girl, Zalia, who had left him and their small daughter when Alicia had still been a baby. She had been killed in a car accident shortly afterwards and now, after six years, he had married again—an English girl. It was a very happy marriage from all accounts, with Alicia devoted to her stepmother Beatrice, who was expecting a baby in the summer.

He drove to a small village some ten miles from Leiden, stopped the car before a solid square house behind high iron railings and got out, opening the door for Jason. His welcome—and Jason's—was warm, and just for a moment he envied his old friend and his pretty wife and little daughter; they were so obviously in love and little Alicia was so happy. His evening was happy too; they spent an hour or so round the fire in the drawing room after dinner—Alicia had gone to bed—Jason and Fred, the van der Eekerk's great dog, heaped together before it.

On the way home the professor addressed Jason, sitting beside him. 'Do you suppose we shall ever find anyone like Beatrice? And if we do shall we snap her up?'

Jason, half-asleep, grumbled gently.

'You agree? Then we had better start looking.'

The next morning, however, such thoughts had no place in the professor's clever head; an early morning walk with Jason was followed by another visit to the hospital, this time to examine patients and give his opinion to his colleagues before going back to his home for lunch.

As for Julie, she had been up early, eaten her breakfast of rolls, slices of cheese, ham and currant bread, drunk a pot of coffee with them, and then, given directions by Mevrouw Schatt, had found her way to St Pieterskerk, where she stayed for the service—not understanding a word, of course. The sermon had gone on for a very long time, but the organ had been magnificent and some of the hymns had sounded very like those at home.

She walked back slowly, looking at the quaint old houses, wishing that she had more time to explore, but the professor had said one o'clock and Mevrouw Schatt had told her that they would eat their lunch at noon.

They got on well together, she and her hostess, who was ready to answer Julie's string of questions about Leiden and its history. Her husband had been something to do with the university, she explained, and she had lived there all her life. She had a great deal to say about everything, but not a word about Professor van der Driesma.

He came at exactly one o'clock, and Julie was ready and waiting for him.

He bade her good afternoon without a smile, passed the time of day with Mevrouw Schatt and asked Julie if she was ready.

'Yes, sir. What am I to do about my bag? Shall I take it with me or am I to fetch it later, before we leave?'

'We shan't leave until early tomorrow morning.' He glanced at his watch and ushered her with speed into the car. The drive was very short indeed, thought Julie; they could have walked in five minutes...

He drove across the forecourt of the hospital and under an arch at one side of the building, parked the car, opened her door and closed it behind her with a snap. 'Through here,' he said, indicating a door.

Julie stood where she was. 'Just a minute, Professor. I think there is something which must be said first.' Her voice shook with rage. 'You bring me here, drive me for miles, dump me, and now you expect me to go with you to some talk or other of which I know nothing. On top of that you alter your plans without bothering to tell me. I had my bag all packed...'

She paused for breath. 'You are a very inconsiderate and tiresome man.' She added coldly, 'Hadn't we better go in? It won't do for you to be late.'

He was standing there looking down at her indignant face. 'It seems that I owe you an apology, Miss Beckworth. I had not realised that you had suffered any discomfort during our journey. Since it is obvious that you feel the need to know exactly what I am doing hour by hour I will do my best to keep you informed. First, however, if you will allow it, we will proceed to the *aula*.'

Put in my place, thought Julie, fuming; he's made me sound like a fussy old woman. I hate him. Without a word she followed him through the door, along a narrow corridor and into the lecture hall, outwardly composed and seething under the composure.

CHAPTER THREE

THE *aula* was packed and they had to walk the length of it to reach the platform where a semicircle of learned-looking men were already sitting. Julie was given a chair beneath it and someone had considerately placed a desk lamp on a small table beside it. There was a tape recorder there too—just in case she couldn't keep up, she supposed. There was also a carafe of water and a glass—in case she felt faint? She smiled at the thought and then composed her features into suitable gravity as a stout, elderly man rose to his feet.

He made a lengthy speech in faultless English, most of it in dignified praise of Professor van der Driesma, who presently rose to his feet and began his lecture. His voice, Julie had to admit, after the rather plummy accents of the stout man, was a pleasure to listen to, and, thank heaven, deliberate enough for her to keep up. When he had finished and invited questions they came thick and fast. It was to be hoped that he wouldn't want the whole lot typed before they left in the morning.

There was an interval then, and someone brought her a cup of tea and a small, feather-light biscuit. She nibbled it slowly and longed for a second cup but it seemed that there weren't going to be any; there were groups of learned-looking men deep in talk and she supposed that for the time being at least there was nothing for her to do. Was she to sit there twiddling

47

her thumbs until the professor came to fetch her or
should she leave? It was less than five minutes' walk
back to Mevrouw Schatt's house...

Professor van der Driesma detached himself from
a group some way away from her and came unhur-
riedly towards her.

'We shall be having discussions for another hour
or so, Miss Beckworth; I have asked someone to show
you to a quiet room so that you can get your notes
typed. I understand there is a very efficient computer
there.' He turned as he spoke and a young man joined
them. 'This is Bas Vliet; he'll show you where to go.
I'll come for you when I'm ready.'

Julie offered a hand. Bas Vliet looked rather nice
so she gave him a brilliant smile and he smiled back.
She switched off the smile when she looked at the
professor. Her 'Very well, sir' was uttered in a re-
signed voice which made him want to shake her.
Anyone less like a downtrodden slave would be hard
to meet, and here she was, the very picture of stoical
servitude. Minx, thought the professor, and walked
away.

'I dare say you have to work hard for the Prof,'
said Bas Vliet sympathetically. 'He never spares
himself and we lesser mortals can't always keep up.'

He opened a door and showed her into a small
office. 'I hope there's everything you'll need here. If
there's anything you want come and find me and I'll
be glad to help.'

Julie thanked him prettily; at first glance there
seemed to be everything she would need. She only
hoped that the professor would remember that she
was there and not go wandering off without her.

'I say, you won't mind if I say that I think you're very pretty?' said Bas. 'The Prof's a lucky man having someone like you working for him.'

Try telling him that, reflected Julie. 'Thank you,' she said demurely. 'I'd better get started...'

He went reluctantly, hoping that he would see her again.

Alone, Julie settled down to work. There was a great deal to get typed up but she was good at her job. All the same it was two hours later that she gathered the sheets together tidily, arranged them with her pen and notebook on the desk and then sat back.

It was almost six o'clock and she was hungry. She thought about supper—a substantial meal, she hoped, and several cups of coffee afterwards. This was a mistake, of course, because she got hungrier, so that when the professor strolled in half an hour later she said crossly, 'There you are. I've been finished for half an hour or more...'

His brows rose. 'You are anxious to return to Mevrouw Schatt?'

'I'm hungry,' said Julie.

'You had tea and a biscuit, surely?'

'Hours ago, and what use is wafer-thin biscuit to someone of my size?'

He said, poker-faced, 'Of no use at all,' and stared at her so fixedly that she blushed.

'We will go now,' he said at length, and held the door for her. 'Be ready to leave at eight o'clock in the morning. I have a lecture at half past nine and shall want you with me. Afterwards I have several patients to see. I shall want you there as I shall make observations for my own use which you will take down in

English.' He added impatiently, 'Now, come along, Miss Beckworth.'

For all the world as though I had kept him waiting, fumed Julie silently.

He left her at Mevrouw Schatt's house after a brief conversation with that lady and an even briefer good-night to herself, and she went thankfully to her room to tidy herself and then down to supper. Thank heaven the Dutch had their evening meal early, she thought, supping delicious soup, then savouring a pork chop with apple sauce and fluffy potatoes and making a contented finish with Dutch apple tart and cream.

Over coffee their desultory conversation merged into a lengthy gossip, while they still sat at the table, until Mevrouw Schatt said, 'You will have to be up early in the morning; you should go to bed, miss.'

'Julie—do call me Julie, please. Yes, I must, but I'll help you with the dishes first; that was a gorgeous meal.'

'You liked?' Mevrouw Schatt was pleased. 'I like to cook and I like also to see what I have cooked eaten with appetite.'

They washed up together in the small, old-fashioned kitchen, and presently Julie went to bed. She hadn't thought about the professor at all; she didn't give him a thought now, but put her bright head on the large, square pillow and went off to sleep.

The professor thumped the knocker at exactly eight o'clock, wished them both a civil good morning, put Julie's case in the boot and opened the car door. There was to be no hanging around . . . She bade Mevrouw Schatt goodbye and promised to write, unhappy that she had no time to buy flowers or a small thank-you gift, but plainly the professor had no intention of lingering. She got into the car and he closed the door on her at once.

'Are we late?' she asked as they drove away.

He glanced at his watch—an elegant, understated gold one on a leather strap. 'No. It is roughly twenty-six miles to Amsterdam. We shall be there in half an hour.'

An insignificant distance, the Bentley made light of it in rather less time.

There was a great deal of traffic on the motorway, which thickened as they passed Schiphol and went on towards the heart of the city. The streets were crowded now, with bicycles as well as cars and trams and buses and people. How they managed to avoid each other seemed a miracle; she decided not to watch the traffic but to look around her. They had left what she took to be an elegant residential area and were driving through narrow streets bordered by canals and narrow, gabled houses, turning away from the main streets.

They had been silent for a long time. She ventured to remark, 'I expect you know your way very well here, Professor?'

'Yes. The hospital is at the end of this street.'

A high wall separated it from the surrounding houses and from the outside at least it looked very old. 'There is an entrance on the other side,' said the professor, 'leading to one of the main streets.'

He was driving across the forecourt; she thought in a panic that she had no idea how long they were to be there or where she was to go.

'How long shall we be here and where am I to go?'

'Until the late afternoon, and you will come with me.'

It was like getting blood out of a stone. 'I wouldn't dream of going off on my own,' said Julie snappily.

He had stopped the car and turned to look at her. 'I would be extremely annoyed if you did, Miss Beckworth.' He added with a sigh, 'After all, I am responsible for you.'

'Oh, pooh,' said Julie, and tossed her bright head. 'You talk as if I were a child.'

His eyes held hers. 'I am very well aware that you are not a child. Come along now!'

The porter had seen them coming and picked up the phone, and by the time they were halfway across the vast entrance hall three persons were coming towards them: an elderly man with a beard and moustache and a jolly face, a younger man with a long, thin face and fair hair already receding from a high domed forehead, and a much younger man who looked awkward.

Everyone shook hands and Julie was introduced and forgot their names at once. They were obviously good friends of the professor, for there was a good deal of laughing and talk, and even the awkward young man joined in. A houseman, she supposed, a registrar and another professor.

'Coffee first,' boomed the older man. 'You will be glad of it I have no doubt, Miss Beckworth, for our good Simon will work you hard, I can assure you.'

He took her arm and led the way along a dark passage and into a rather grand room full of gentlemen with coffee-cups in their hands. They surged forward to greet the professor, who introduced her once more with a wave of the hand. 'My secretary, Miss Beckworth.' It was a signal for several of the younger men present to offer her cups of coffee, and presently the professor joined her. 'A sister will be here in a moment to show you where you can do your typing if you should have time to spare, and where you can put your jacket and so on.'

As long as there's a loo, thought Julie, following a placid-looking nurse down another dark passage. The room wasn't far away, and thank heaven there was a cloakroom next door. 'I will wait for you,' said the sister, and smiled. 'When the professor has finished his lecture I will fetch you from the lecture hall and show you where you can have your lunch.'

'You will? That's awfully kind.' Julie nipped smartly away, made sure that she had everything she needed with her and then rejoined her guide.

Most of the men had gone from the room when they returned but the professor was still there, deep in conversation with the elderly man who had met them. The young man was there too, hovering anxiously.

'Ready?' The professor was brisk. 'Come along, then.' He paused to say something to the sister, who smiled at him and made a quiet reply before he ushered Julie out of the room.

They all walked out of the passage and into a wide corridor and through a door at its end. There was a large lecture hall beyond; a sea of faces turned to look at them as they went in. Julie was ushered to a seat at the end of the front row and the others climbed onto the platform. She wondered if it was going to be the same lecture as the one he had given at Leiden; if so, that would make things easier for her.

It wasn't; it was all about haemorrhagic diseases—purpura and thrombocytopenia—and he was full of long medical words which taxed her intelligence and speed to their utmost. He had an awful lot to say about them too, and afterwards there were questions and answers. When he finally sat down she laid down her pencil with a shaking hand and heaved a sigh of relief.

There was a young woman sitting next to her. She turned to Julie now. 'You have noted every word?' she wanted to know. 'Is he not splendid? You must be proud to work for him. He is a brilliant man and much revered.'

The girl had an earnest face with lank hair and large spectacles.

'You're a doctor?' asked Julie politely.

'I am qualified, yes, but I have much to learn. I wish to be as clever as Professor van der Driesma; there is no one equal to him.'

She looked at Julie so accusingly that she made haste to agree. 'Oh, yes, he is a very clever man...' She paused because the girl had gone very red and was looking at someone behind Julie's shoulder.

The professor said quietly, 'There is someone come to take you to your lunch, Miss Beckworth.' And then to the girl he said, 'You enjoyed the lecture? I do hope so; it is a most interesting subject.'

'Yes, yes, Professor, I listened to every word. I have told your secretary what a brilliant man you are and she agrees with me...'

The professor covered a small sound with a cough. 'I am flattered. You are recently qualified?' he asked kindly. 'I wish you a successful future.'

They left the girl then and walked back along the corridor to where she saw the same sister waiting, but before they reached her he observed, 'There is no need to bolster my ego, Miss Beckworth; I feel sure that you consider that it is already grossly swollen.'

'Well, really,' said Julie. 'Whatever will you say next?'

'What is more to the point—what will you say, Miss Beckworth?'

She said suddenly, 'I do wish you would stop calling me Miss Beckworth; it makes me feel middle-aged and plain and dull...'

'Perhaps that is how I wish to think of you. Please be ready to accompany me to the wards at two o'clock. You will be fetched. You have all you need in the office?'

He said a word to the sister and went past them down the corridor. The sister said, 'If you will come with me? We have a dining room—a canteen, you call it?' She glanced at her watch. 'You have time to eat and then work before two o'clock.'

Julie walked beside her to the lifts and was taken down to the basement where she collected a bowl of soup, a salad, rolls, butter and cold meat and sat down with her guide, and all the time she wondered why the professor thought of her as plain and middle-aged. He must dislike me very much, she reflected; perhaps when they got back to St Bravo's she should apply for a transfer.

By two o'clock she had typed up more than half her notes and she had taken the precaution of going to the cloakroom to do her face and tidy her hair so that when the same sister came back she was ready. A good thing, for she was hurried along at a great rate through a warren of passages and in and out of lifts. 'We must not keep the professor waiting,' said her companion anxiously.

At the ward doors she was handed over to the ward sister, who smiled and nodded; there was no time to

do more; the professor, wearing his glasses, a stetho-
scope slung round his shoulders and a preoccupied
look, came into the ward with the three men who had
met them when they had arrived.

He shook hands with Sister, saying something to
make her laugh, nodded to Julie, who gave him a
wooden stare, and went to the first bed.

He spent several minutes talking to the young
woman lying in it, which gave Julie time to study him
at her leisure. He had, she conceded, a nice face—
the word 'nice' covering a variety of things: good
looks, the kind of nose which could be looked down
with shattering effect and a thin mouth which could
break into a charming smile. Despite the good looks,
it was a man's face to be trusted. She wondered if one
could trust someone who didn't like you and whom
you didn't like either...

He looked up suddenly, staring at her across the
bed, and she blushed, in a sudden panic that he had
said something and she hadn't been listening. He
hadn't, but after that she had no time to think about
anything but the necessity of getting his comments
down correctly. And since they were intersected by
discussions in Dutch she had to keep her wits about
her.

Altogether a tiring afternoon, she decided when
finally he finished the round and went away with his
companions and Sister. Leaving me here to get lost,
I suppose, thought Julie, longing for a cup of tea—
a whole pot of tea. She was roused from this gloomy
thought by a tap on the arm. The same sister who
had been her guide all day was there again.

'Tea?' she asked. 'In the sisters' sitting room; we
shall be so pleased to see you.'

'Oh, I'd love that.' Julie beamed at her. 'But oughtn't I to let Professor van der Driesma know?'

'It is he who has arranged that you should have tea with us.'

'Really? Well, in that case, I'll come now, shall I?'

The nurses' home was attached to the hospital—a modern block built behind the main building—and the room she was ushered into was large and comfortable and fairly full of young women in uniform.

They welcomed her warmly, telling her their names, asking her if she had enjoyed her visit to the hospital, sitting her in one of the easy chairs, offering tea. 'With milk and sugar, just as Professor van der Driesma asked,' explained one pretty girl. '"English tea," he told us, "and there must be cake and not little biscuits!"'

'Oh, did he say that?' Julie felt guilty and mean—all her unkind thoughts of him not bothering about her and he had remembered about the biscuits. Oh, dear...!

She drank several cups of tea and ate the cake— *boterkoek*, a kind of madeira cake but buttery and without the lemon—and she answered the questions fired at her. They all spoke English, some better than others, and several of the girls there had been to England on holiday. An hour passed pleasantly until someone glanced at the clock and she was bustled away amid a chorus of goodbyes.

'The Professor must not be kept waiting,' was followed by another chorus of *tot ziens*.

'That means see you soon,' said her guide, racing up and down passages very much in the same manner as the white rabbit in *Alice in Wonderland*.

Julie caught up with her in the lift. 'Are you all scared of the professor?' she asked.

'Scared? No, no. We like him very much, therefore we do everything to please him. He is a good man and his heart is warm.'

Julie blinked. This was an aspect of him which she hadn't so far encountered. She must try and remember it next time he chilled her with an icy stare.

She collected her notebooks and typing, got her jacket and, urged on by her companion, went to the entrance. The professor was there, talking to the man with the beard, his hands in his pockets, looking as though he meant to stand there chatting for some time, but he glanced round as they reached him. 'Ready? You haven't forgotten anything?' He said something in Dutch to the sister and shook her hand before bidding the bearded gentleman goodbye, and then waited while the latter took Julie's hand and said that he hoped to see her again.

'You have seen nothing of our lovely city, Miss Beckworth; it is a pity that Simon has no time to take you sightseeing.'

Julie allowed her eyelashes to sweep her cheeks before glancing up at the whiskered face. 'Oh, but I'm here to work,' she said demurely. 'But I hope to come back one day and explore on my own.'

'My dear young lady, I am sure you would not be on your own for long.'

Julie smiled charmingly. 'Well, I dare say I would bring someone with me to keep me company.'

The professor coughed and she said quickly, 'I'm wasting time, I'm afraid. I must say goodbye—no, what is it you say? *Tot ziens.*'

The professor had opened the car door and she got in, and after a brief conversation with his colleague he got in beside her.

'Where to?' asked Julie flippantly.

'Groningen. We shall be there for tomorrow and the greater part of the following day before we return to Leiden, where I have patients to see. You will lodge with Mevrouw Schatt again and we shall return to England on the day after that.'

'I expect you're tired,' said Julie sweetly. She wasn't surprised when he didn't answer her.

They were leaving Amsterdam behind when he said, 'Look at the map. We are going north-east to Groningen. The first town is Naarden, then Amersfoort; just past Harderwijk we will stop for a meal. A pity there is no time to use the less busy road; I'm afraid it must be motorway for the whole way.'

They had driven for little more than forty minutes when he turned off the motorway and took a side-road winding through woodlands. 'We have had a busy day,' he said. 'We deserve a leisurely dinner.' Then he drove between two stone pillars onto a drive which led to a hotel ringed around by trees and shrubs.

Julie peered around her; it looked a splendid place and she hoped that her clothes would live up to its magnificence. She was given no time to brood over this, however, but was swept in through its doors, pointed in the direction of the cloakroom and told that he would be waiting for her in the foyer.

He sounded impatient beneath the cool good manners and she whisked away, intent on making the best of things. The cloakroom was luxurious, full of mirrors and pale pink washbasins and with a shelf of toiletries. One could, she supposed, if one had time, shampoo one's hair, give oneself a manicure, try out a variety of lipsticks . . . It was tempting but the professor mustn't be kept waiting.

The restaurant was elegant and almost full, but the table the *maitre d'* led them to was in one of the wide windows with a view of the small lake half-hidden by trees. 'Oh, how very pretty! Do you come here often?'

'Occasionally. You would like a sherry while we order?'

His manner, she thought wistfully, was exactly the same as when he sat behind his desk dictating letters. 'Please.' She accepted the menu that she was offered and began to work her way through it. There was a great deal of it and the prices made her feel quite faint. Still, if he could afford it . . . On the other hand, out of consideration for his pocket she should choose those dishes which weren't quite so costly. Soup, she decided, and an omelette.

The professor's quiet voice cut into her pondering. 'The lobster mousseline with champagne sauce is an excellent starter, and how about duckling with orange sauce to follow? Merely a suggestion, of course.'

A suggestion that she was only too happy to agree to, and she sat quietly while he conferred with the wine waiter, looking around her. The women there were well-dressed and the men looked prosperous; it was nice to see how the other half lived.

The lobster was everything that the professor had said of it and she didn't know much about wines, but the white wine she was offered was delicious, pale and dry; she drank it sparingly and so did he. The duckling when it came was mouthwateringly crisp with its orange sauce, straw potatoes and baby sprouts.

While they ate they talked—by no means an animated conversation but easy, casual talk, with not a word about themselves or the day's work. Julie turned her attention to the toffee pudding with a light heart.

They didn't sit over their coffee; it was already dark and there were still, he informed her, more than eighty miles to drive. 'Another hour and a half's drive,' he observed, opening the car door for her.

It was too dark to see much of the countryside now, but as he slowed through the few villages on the motorway she craned her neck to see as much as possible. The road bypassed a big town too, brightly lighted and busy with local traffic. When they reached Assen, the professor said, 'Not long now. We will go straight to the hospital. You will sleep there and accompany me in the morning to the seminar. International.'

'Everyone will speak English, I hope?'

'Oh, yes, with a variety of accents.'

Groningen, when they reached it, looked charming under the streetlamps. The professor drove straight to the heart of the city, crossing first one square and then a second. 'All the main streets lead off from these two squares,' he explained. 'The hospital is down this side-street.'

It was a splendid building with a vast entrance hall, where she wasn't allowed to linger. The professor spoke to the porter and crossed to the row of lifts, taking her with him. 'My bag,' said Julie, hurrying to keep up.

'It will be taken to your room. Come along now, and I'll introduce you to the warden who will take care of you.'

'At what time do you want me to start work, Professor?' She was facing him in the lift. 'And how shall I know where to find you?'

'You will be fetched at half past eight. The seminar starts at nine with a coffee interval and a break for lunch. You will be shown where you can have a meal. We start again at two o'clock and finish around four. I hope to leave here not later than two o'clock on the day after tomorrow. Then you will spend the night with Mevrouw Schatt, and be free in the morning.'

The lift had stopped. 'Thank you, Professor; it's nice to know your plans. I'll be ready in the morning.'

He didn't answer but she hadn't expected him to. Why waste words when one or even none would do? He marched her along a corridor then over a covered bridge to a building behind the hospital and knocked on a door at the end of the passage. It was opened by an elderly woman in a sister's uniform who smiled at him and shook hands. 'Zuster Moerma, this is Miss Beckworth, my secretary; I know you'll look after her.'

Julie shook hands and then waited while the two of them engaged in a brief conversation in Dutch. That finished, the professor bade her goodnight, turned on his heel and went away.

Zuster Moerma watched him go. 'Such a kind man,' she observed. 'Now you will come with me, please, and I will show you your room. Someone will bring you a warm drink—tea, perhaps? You must be tired; the professor works hard and he expects everyone else to do the same.'

Julie's room was small, nicely furnished and pleasantly warm. She was bidden goodnight, assured that breakfast would be brought to her at half past seven next morning, that the bathroom was just across

the passage and that a tray of tea would be brought
to her in a few minutes.

Someone had brought her bag and computer up to
the room; she unpacked what she would need and put
the computer on the solid little table by the window.
She still had half an hour's typing to do. The professor, being the man he was, would probably ask for
it the moment he saw her in the morning.

The tea-tray came, borne by a cheerful girl in a print
dress and white pinny. Old-fashioned but nice, thought
Julie, and settled down to enjoy a cup. There were
biscuits too—thin, crisp and sweet. She wasn't hungry
but she ate some of them before having a bath and
settling down at the table to finish her typing.

She was sleepy by the time she got into bed, and
closed her eyes at once with only a fleeting thought
of the professor. Probably buried under a pile of
papers with those glasses on his nose, she thought,
only half-awake.

The same girl brought her breakfast in the morning.
Julie had been up since seven o'clock and had
showered and dressed; now she sat down to enjoy the
coffee and rolls with the little dish of cheese and ham
which accompanied them, and, her meal over, she
carefully checked everything, packed her bag once
more and put the computer into its case. She had no
idea if she would have time to do any work before
they left but doubtless the professor would tell her.
He had, she conceded, been careful to keep her up to
date with his plans.

Zuster Moerma came for her at half past eight
exactly and led her back into the hospital. Julie, following on her heels, lost all sense of direction before

long. The various staircases they went up and down
all looked alike, as did the corridors. She could hear
sounds of activity coming from the various doors they
passed—the wards, she supposed.

The *aula* was reached finally; it was larger than in
Leiden and filled to capacity with rows of serious-
looking gentlemen. Professor van der Driesma was
standing by the door as they reached it and bade them
good morning, exchanged what Julie supposed were
a few pleasantries with Zuster Moerma, then turned
to Julie.

'They've given you a table under the platform so
that you can hear easily. There will be a good deal of
discussion.'

An understatement, thought Julie an hour later;
there had been a great deal of discussion and she had
had to keep her wits about her, and there was still
another hour after the coffee-break. Much refreshed
by the brimming mug that someone had brought her,
she bent once more over her pad.

A nurse led her away for her lunch in the canteen. A
pretty girl with fair hair and big blue eyes, with the
unlikely name of Skutsje, which Julie was quite unable
to pronounce correctly. She wasn't from Groningen
but her home was in Friesland, just across the county
border. 'I work here now,' she explained in awkward
English, 'and it is very nice.'

Julie shared a table with her and several other
nurses; all of them had a smattering of English, and
plied her with questions over their bowls of soup and
Kaas broodjes, and she wished that she could have
seen more of them, but, anxious not to be late, she
was led back to the *aula* to find the professor already

there, talking to a small group of colleagues. He nodded to her as she went to her seat and presently came over to her.

'You have had lunch?' he wanted to know. 'When this session is finished you will have time to type up your notes, will you not? Tomorrow morning you will be free; I have consultations until lunchtime. I should like to leave here directly after that. Shall we meet in the entrance hall just before two o'clock?'

'Very well, Professor. You mean I can do as I like until then?'

'Certainly. I dare say you will want to look at the shops, and St Martiniskerk is well worth a visit. I'm sorry you have had no chance to look around Groningen today.'

'Well, I came to work, didn't I?' said Julie cheerfully. 'But I shall enjoy looking round tomorrow morning. I'll be in the hall on time.'

'Good.' He went away then and left her to settle herself down, ready for the afternoon's work. Various medical men were reading papers and she had to keep her mind on her work. There was a brief break for a cup of tea but then they were off again, and since they were from a variety of countries she was hard put to it to keep up with some of their accented English. She was glad that she had a tape recorder with her to fill in the gaps.

She didn't see the professor again but went away with Skutsje, who had come to fetch her to a small office where she could get on with her typing. That lasted till she was fetched once more to eat her supper—a cheerful meal with the nurses whom she had met at midday. Afterwards, despite their friendly offers to take her with them to watch TV in their sitting room, she went back to the office to finish her work.

It was quite late by the time she had typed the last of the notes; she tidied the pile of paper, collected her belongings and found her way back to the nurses' home where she showered and got into bed, to sleep at once. It had been a long and arduous day and she only hoped that she hadn't missed anything.

The morning was bright and crisply cold; she ate her breakfast while she was told where to go and what to see and presently left the hospital on her sightseeing tour, promising to be back for the midday meal. She went first to St Martiniskerk, admired the beautiful frescos, listened to the carillon and decided that she hadn't the time to climb the three hundred and twenty feet to the top of the Martini Tower.

A morning wasn't long enough, she decided, taking a quick look at the university and the gardens in the Prinsenhof before finding the shops so that she could buy presents to take home. She hadn't much money; she settled for illustrated books for her brothers, some chocolates for Esme, cigars for Luscombe and a small delft plate for her mother. Blotto would have to have biscuits.

That done, it was time for her to take herself back to the hospital and go to the canteen for soup and rolls and salad. Lunch was fun, with everyone talking at once, until she saw the time, regretfully said goodbye and hurried over to the home to get her things.

The warden met her. The porter had already taken everything, she was told, and then she was bidden a warm goodbye. She shook hands with the hope that

she would come again some day and made her way
to the entrance hall; it was ten minutes to the hour
and she intended to be the first one there. There was
no one in the hall and the porter in his box had his
back to her. There was no sign of her bag and the
computer either; she crossed to the big entrance door
and looked out.

The professor was there, standing by his car, talking
to a girl. Even at that distance Julie could see that
she was strikingly good-looking and beautifully
dressed. As she looked he put his arms around her
shoulders and kissed her, and then, an arm in hers,
walked her across the forecourt to a scarlet Mini. The
girl got in and he bent once more to kiss her and then
stood watching as she drove away.

Julie went back to where the lifts were without the
porter seeing her, and a moment later the professor
came into the hall; she started to walk towards him.
'I'm not late?' she asked as they met.

He was coolly polite. 'Exactly on time, Miss
Beckworth.' She found it impossible to believe that
he was the same man who had hugged the girl
so closely.

CHAPTER FOUR

THE professor drove straight to Mevrouw Schatt's house when they reached Leiden. 'I have an appointment shortly but I would be obliged if you will come to the hospital in about an hour's time. I have a number of letters to dictate. You can get them typed there and I will sign them before I leave the hospital.'

He stayed for a few minutes talking to Mevrouw Schatt before getting back into his car and driving away, and Julie went to her room and presently returned downstairs for a cup of tea and some of Mevrouw Schatt's *boterkoek*, while she told that lady of her visits to Amsterdam and Groningen. An hour wasn't long, though, and she got into her jacket once more and walked to the hospital. She was relieved that the porter expected her and summoned another porter to take her to Professor van der Driesma's office.

He was sitting behind a big desk, loaded down with papers, his specs on his nose, but he got up as she went in, asked her to sit down, hoped that she had had time for tea and began without more ado on his letters.

Most of them were straightforward, she was thankful to discover—courtesy thanks for this and that, arrangements to meet in London, agreements to consultations—only a handful were bristling with medical terms.

'Bring them here when you have finished, please, Miss Beckworth; I will see you back to Mevrouw Schatt's house then.'

'Please don't bother,' said Julie. 'It's only a few minutes' walk; you must have heaps of other things to do.'

'Indeed I have, but I must remind you that I am responsible for you, Miss Beckworth.'

Julie stood up and gathered up her pad and pencil and the little medical dictionary that she was never without. 'Oh, dear, so tiresome for you, Professor. I'll be as quick as I can.'

He got up to open the door for her and stood watching her walk away along the corridor. A pity that she didn't turn round to see him, and see the look on his face.

She went to the office that she had used before and wasted quite five minutes of her time thinking about him and the girl in the hospital courtyard. He had looked, even at a distance, loving, and for some reason the thought made her feel vaguely unhappy. She thrust it aside and switched on the computer. I ought to feel pleased that he's human like the rest of us, after all, she reflected.

She doubted that when she returned with his letters; the quick look he gave her as she laid them on his desk was coolly indifferent. As though he's looking at me over a high wall, thought Julie; if she hadn't seen him kissing that girl she wouldn't have believed it...

She looked at his downbent head as he signed his letters. Perhaps he was unhappy without her; perhaps for some reason they weren't able to marry; perhaps the girl was already married... Julie's imagination set off on a wild-goose chase of its own, to be interrupted by his quiet 'Miss Beckworth, if I might have your attention?'

She gave him a guilty look. 'Yes, yes, of course, Professor.'

'You have had no time to yourself while we have been in Holland; when we get back to London you might like to have a day to yourself before coming back to work?'

'Thank you, sir. I still have some notes to write up, though.'

He said indifferently, 'Just as you like. I expect you can arrange your work to suit yourself, but I shan't need you for the first day after our return.' He signed the last letter. 'You are ready? Let us go.'

He didn't wait at *mevrouw's* house but saw her inside and drove off quickly. Siska and Jason would be waiting to welcome him home on the other side of Rapenburg.

They were expecting him; Siska had the door open as he got out of the car and Jason hurled himself at him. The professor closed his front door behind him and thought how delightful it was to be home, and for the first time in many years he thought, too, how pleasant it would be if he had a wife waiting for him. Someone like Julie, who unfortunately had made it very plain from the beginning that she didn't like him.

He shrugged the thought aside, bent to caress his dog, listened to Siska's domestic gossip and went along to his study. There was time enough for him to catch up on his letters before dinner.

He took Jason for a walk later that evening but he didn't cross to the other side of the canal; he could see that the only light on at her house was an upstairs one and, in any case, what would be the point?

He was up early the next morning, taking Jason for his run then going over to the hospital for a brief examination of the patients whom he had gone to see previously. He would go back again to bid his colleagues goodbye before he left later in the day. Now he went back to his house to his study to telephone, and then into his drawing room to drink the coffee that Siska had ready from him.

The long windows overlooked the street, which was free from traffic and quiet in the autumn morning. Indeed, there was only one person in it—Julie, walking briskly towards the Rapenburg, probably on her way back from another visit to St Pieterskerk and the Persijnhofje—an almshouse founded by an ancestor of President Franklin Roosevelt—and doubtless on her way to another museum. It was a windy day and she had stopped to pin back her hair; on a sudden impulse he went to the house door and opened it and, as she drew level, her head bowed against the wind, went down the double steps.

'Good morning, Miss Beckworth. You're out early. Come in and have a cup of coffee?'

She gaped up at him. 'Oh, hello. I didn't expect ... That is, are you staying in one of these houses?' She looked around her. 'Do they belong to the university?'

'Some of them do. Come inside; this wind is chilly.'

She went indoors with him and Siska, carrying the coffee-tray, came into the hall. The professor spoke to her, took Julie's jacket and then led the way into his drawing room, where Jason came to inspect her, rolling his yellow eyes and showing a splendid set of teeth.

Julie held out a fist and hoped that he wouldn't devour it, but he didn't; at a quiet word from the professor he butted his great head against it and leered at her in what could only be a friendly fashion. 'He's yours? You live here?' asked Julie.

'Yes, and yes. This is one of my homes, although I do spend a good deal of time in London.'

She looked around her; the room was large and high-ceilinged, its walls hung with mulberry-coloured paper. The floor was polished wood, covered by beautiful rugs, and the furniture was mahogany and tulip wood: a lovely William and Mary chest, a bureau of the same period, heavy with marquetry, a Dutch display cabinet, its shelves filled with silver and porcelain, and a sofa-table behind a vast couch. There were tripod tables too, each with its lamp, and here and there superb Meissen porcelain figures.

'What a very beautiful room,' said Julie.

'I'm glad you like it. Come and sit down and have your coffee.'

Julie sat down and drank her coffee from a paper-thin porcelain cup and nibbled little cinnamon biscuits, making polite conversation and feeling ill at ease. The professor behind his desk or lecturing in his quiet voice was one thing; drinking his coffee in his splendid house was quite another.

He responded to her rather vapid remarks with un-wonted gentleness and hidden amusement, egging her on gently to talk about her family and home so that she forgot her uncertainty towards him, again talking freely about her father.

She paused at length, suddenly shy and afraid that she had been rambling on and boring him. 'I must go,' she said. 'Mevrouw Schatt will be waiting for me. I'm sorry, I've wasted your morning; there must be so much you want to do when you're home...' She remembered something. 'I expect you have friends—and people you know in Groningen...'

'Indeed I have, for I was born there; my family live there, and people I have known for many years.'

She asked recklessly, 'So you don't want to go back there and—and settle down?'

'I imagine, Miss Beckworth, that you mean do I wish to marry and live there.' He studied her pink face before he went on. 'This is my true home; if and when I decide to marry, my wife will live here.'

Julie got to her feet. 'Yes, of course; I'm sorry, I wasn't prying. Thank you for the coffee.'

He went into the hall with her and picked up a jacket, calling something to his housekeeper. 'I'm going over to the hospital for half an hour. We may as well walk together.'

Jason went with them, keeping close to his master, the epitome of a well-mannered dog—curling his lip at a cat sitting on a window-sill, growling at a passing poodle on its lead, but obedient to the professor's quiet voice. They crossed the Rapenburg and paused outside Mevrouw Schatt's house.

'I will be here at two o'clock,' he reminded her. 'I wish to be back in London by the evening.'

Mevrouw Schatt had taken great pains with their meal: enormous pancakes filled with crisp bacon, swimming in syrup, a salad and something which looked and tasted like a blancmange and which she called *pudding*. There was a glass of milk too and, to finish, coffee. Julie, uncertain as to when she would have the next meal, enjoyed it all.

Mindful of the professor's wish to leave on time, she fetched her things from her room, gave Mevrouw Schatt the box of chocolates that she had bought that morning and got into her jacket. It had turned much colder during the last day or two and she stuffed a scarf and gloves into its pockets, made sure that her hair was bandbox-neat and sat down to wait. Not for long! The big car drew up silently outside the front door and the professor banged the knocker.

His conversation with Mevrouw Schatt was brief and cordial; her bag and computer were put into the boot and she was invited to get into the car. Julie embraced Mevrouw Schatt, sorry to leave her kind hostess, and did as she was asked, sitting silently until they were clear of the town and on the motorway. 'Did Jason mind your leaving?' she asked at length.

'Yes, but I shall be coming over again very shortly. Not to work, though.'

To see that girl, thought Julie, and felt a sudden shaft of sadness at the thought.

Their journey back went smoothly. They stopped briefly in Ghent for tea and then drove on to Calais and a rather choppy crossing to Dover. Approaching London, Julie stared out at the dreary suburbs and wished herself back in Leiden, but when the professor observed idly, 'You will be glad to be home again, Miss Beckworth,' she was quick to agree.

'Although I enjoyed seeing something of Holland,' she told him, and went on awkwardly, 'Thank you for arranging everything so well for me, sir.'

His reply was non-committal and most unsatisfactory. Their rare moments of pleasure in each other's society were already forgotten, she supposed.

He drove her straight home despite her protests. 'And take the day off tomorrow,' he told her. 'Any work you still have to do you can doubtless fit in later on.'

She murmured an assent; there *was* a backlog of work, despite her best efforts; she would go in early tomorrow morning and clear up what work was outstanding and then take the rest of the day off. He wouldn't know, for he had said that he wouldn't be needing her for a day. Doubtless he would take a day off too.

Rather cautiously, she asked him if he would like to come in for a cup of coffee when they reached her home. His refusal was polite and tinged with impatience, and she wasted no time in getting out of the car when he opened her door, took her bag and set it in the porch, before driving away with the remark that he would see her in a day's time. Luscombe opened the door as he drove away.

'Welcome home, Miss Julie—he's in a hurry, isn't he?'

'I expect he's going straight to the hospital, Luscombe.' She bent to pat Blotto. 'It's lovely to be home; where's Mother?'

'In the garden with Esme, sweeping up the leaves. They didn't expect you so early. Like a pot of tea? The kettle is on the boil.'

'I'd love one, Luscombe; I'll go and surprise them . . .'

'You do that, Miss Julie; we've had supper but I'll find something tasty for you—half an hour do?'

'Lovely—I'm famished. We seem to have been driving for ever; it seems later than it is.'

She went through the house and out into the garden. The light outside the kitchen door shone on her mother and sister, muffled against the chilly evening, busy with their rakes. They threw them down when they saw her.

'Julie, how lovely; you didn't say exactly when you'd be back on your card.' Her mother laughed. 'That's why we're here working in the dark. We wanted the garden to be spick and span when you got back.'

Esme had flung down her rake. 'Did he bring you back? The professor?'

'Yes, but he didn't want to stop. He's given me the day off tomorrow.'

'Quite right too,' said her mother. 'Were you kept very busy?'

'Yes, but I did manage to see Leiden and Groningen.'

They had all gone inside, and over the supper that Luscombe had conjured up she gave them an account of her few days in Holland.

'Liked it, did you?' asked Luscombe, leaning against the door with a dishcloth over one arm. 'Meet anyone nice, did you?'

'Any number of people, but only briefly; almost all the time I was either taking notes or typing them.'

'Well, you can have a nice, quiet day tomorrow,' observed Mrs Beckworth. She peered at her daughter thoughtfully. 'You didn't go out at all, I suppose? Or see much of Professor van der Driesma?'

'Only at the seminars and his ward rounds.' Julie paused. 'Oh, and he came out of his house as I went past it in Leiden and he asked me in for coffee.'

'He lives there? As well as here? He's married?'

'No, not as far as I know.' Julie sounded casual. 'I must go in to work in the morning. I'll go early—I've some audio typing to finish. A couple of hours will see to it and then I'll come home and we'll do something special—a film, perhaps? Or lunch out? I haven't spent a penny so I'll treat.'

'Let's go to a film,' begged Esme. 'It's ages since we went...'

'All right. We could go in the afternoon and have tea somewhere afterwards.' Julie went into the hall and fetched her bag. 'I didn't have time to do much shopping,' she explained, handing over her small gifts.

'You didn't ought,' said Luscombe, beaming at his box of cigars.

It was lovely being home, reflected Julie, and then frowned at the unbidden image of the professor's face which floated behind her eyelids. Why I should think about him, I don't know.

Probably because he was thinking about her. There was nothing romantic about his thoughts, however, rather a vague annoyance. He found her disturbing, prone to answer back—even though she was a first-rate worker, melting, as far as possible, into the background but always at hand. Despite this he was always aware of her.

She had, as it were, cast a spanner into the works of his life. He would probably have to get rid of her—nicely, of course. He had no intention of allowing any deep feelings to alter his life. He was no monk, but beyond mild flirtation with one or other of his women acquaintances he had remained heart-whole. Not that his heart was involved now, he reflected; he merely found her disturbing.

Julie was at her desk soon after eight o'clock; she had got up early, shared a cup of tea and some toast with Luscombe and caught a bus well before the rush hour started. She had her earphones on, transcribing the last of the tapes, when a hand fell on her shoulder; the other hand removed her headphones.

'I thought I had told you to take a day off, Miss Beckworth.' The professor's voice had a nasty edge to it.

'So you did, but you didn't say I wasn't to come into the office,' said Julie reasonably. 'I had quite a bit of work to finish, you know, and you know as well as I do that I'll never get a chance to fit it in once we're back here.'

She turned in her chair to look at him. 'I'll be finished in less than half an hour. I didn't think you would be here. Aren't you taking a day off too?'

Staring down at her lovely smiling face, the professor gave way to a sudden, ridiculous impulse.

'Yes, Miss Beckworth. Like you, I came in to finish some paperwork. But I have the rest of the day in which to do nothing. Shall we give ourselves a rest and spend the day in the country? I think that we both deserve it.'

'Me and you?' said Julie, not mincing her words. 'Well, I never... That is, thank you very much, Professor, but I promised that I'd take my mother and sister out.'

'Better still. Perhaps they would like to come too?'

A remark which disappointed her. She squashed the feeling at once. 'Well, I'm sure they'd like that very much. Where do you want to go?'

'Supposing we let your sister decide, or at least suggest somewhere?'

He's lonely, Julie thought suddenly. I dare say he's missing that girl and can't bear to be on his own. 'If I could have twenty minutes to finish this?'

'I'll be outside when you're ready.'

I must be mad, reflected Julie, making no effort to get on with her work. And what on earth are we going to talk about? They had driven miles in Holland exchanging barely a word between them ...

He was waiting by the car when she left the hospital and as she came towards him he wondered if he had taken leave of his senses. Nothing of that showed on his face as he opened the car door for her to get in.

Mrs Beckworth opened the door as they reached it. 'Oh, good, you're back, Julie. Professor van der Driesma, come in; I'm just making coffee.' She gave him her hand and smiled up at him; whatever Julie said, Mrs Beckworth thought that he was a very nice man—that mild description covering her entire approval.

'Professor van der Driesma suggested that as he was free we might like to join him for a drive into the country.'

'Oh, how delightful.' Mrs Beckworth raised her voice. 'Esme, come here, love; something delightful ...'

Esme came downstairs two at a time and landed up against the professor.

'Hello,' she said in a pleased voice. 'You're not going away again, are you? There are a lot of things I want to know.'

He smiled down at her. Why doesn't he smile at me like that? thought Julie.

'Are there? Perhaps I'll have time to answer them. We wondered, your sister and I, if you and your mother would like to come for a drive...?'

'With you? In your car? Oh, yes, yes. Where shall we go? And can we go now?'

'Coffee first,' said Mrs Beckworth, 'and you'll tidy yourself before you set foot outside the door, Esme.'

There was a general move towards the kitchen, where Luscombe was pouring coffee. He had, of course, been listening. 'Going off for the day?' he wanted to know. 'Suits me a treat; I'll pop over to my sister's if it's all the same to you, Mrs Beckworth.'

'Yes, do go, Luscombe. I don't know when we shall be back...' She looked at the professor, sitting opposite her at the kitchen table.

'Oh, after tea, if that suits you, Mrs Beckworth.' He turned to Esme, perched beside him. 'Where shall we go, Esme?'

'Brighton—oh, please say we can. Sally, my best friend, says it's super. The Lanes, all the shops and the Pavilion.'

'Why not? But we'll go the long way round to get there, shall we? We have all day. Supposing we go there in the afternoon and have tea there?'

Esme flung her arms round his neck and kissed him. 'Oh, you really are very nice,' she told him. 'May I sit with you so's I can ask you questions?'

'I shall be delighted.'

'Esme, you must allow Professor van der Driesma to decide where we are to go.' Mrs Beckworth sounded apologetic. 'I'm sorry, Professor, Esme's excited; we don't often get treats like this.'

'Nor do I, Mrs Beckworth, and I have a sixteen-year-old sister.'

'Have you? You must miss your family.'

'I do, although I don't see much of them whether I am here or in Holland.'

Julie had sat quietly drinking her coffee; now she said, 'Shall we go and get our things, Esme?' And when she and her mother and Esme had left the room the professor collected up the mugs and took them over to the sink.

'You worked for Dr Beckworth, of course,' he said to Luscombe. 'He was a good man and a splendid doctor.'

'Yer right there. Started 'ere when Miss Julie was a little nipper—general dogsbody, as you might say, till I took over the 'ousekeeping, like. The doctor would expect me to stay on and keep an eye on the ladies.'

'I'm sure he couldn't have picked a better man, Luscombe. Can we drop you off on our way?'

'Well, now, if you could spare ten minutes while I tidy meself a bit. I'd better take Blotto with me.'

'No need. He can come with us; there's plenty of room in the car. Where do you want to go, Luscombe?'

'The Whitechapel road, just this side of Fenchurch Street Station; me sister's got a fish and chip shop.'

'Splendid. I intend to cross the river; I can go over London Bridge.'

'You know your way around, then?' He glanced round the kitchen. 'Everything's shipshape.' He glanced at a peacefully sleeping dog. 'Sure you don't mind about Blotto?'

'Not in the least.' The professor turned to smile at Esme, her hair combed and plaited, in a pleated skirt and short jacket. 'Luscombe's coming as far as his sister's. We'll take Blotto with us, shall we?'

'Oh, please. We ought to have asked you; I'm sorry, but you see we weren't expecting you. Were you feeling rather lonely for your family in Holland?'

'I had no time to visit them. I'll be going back shortly, though.'

'Will they come and visit you at your house? Julie said you had a lovely old house near the hospital. Why don't you—?' She was interrupted by her mother's entry.

'Professor—oh, must I keep calling you that? What are we to do with Blotto? He'll have to go with Luscombe...'

'Call me Simon, Mrs Beckworth, and Blotto is coming with us.'

'I'll get his lead.' Esme flew away as Julie joined them, and a moment later so did Luscombe, in his best jacket and with his hair slicked down.

'You've got your key, Luscombe?' asked Mrs Beckworth. 'I've got mine. Don't hurry back; we'll be quite all right.'

'Right-o, Mrs Beckworth; I've locked up.'

The professor ushered his party out to the car and settled them with Luscombe in front and Blotto on Julie's knee. He was beginning to enjoy himself although he couldn't think why.

There was a small queue outside Luscombe's sister's shop and they turned as one to stare as he got out of the car. 'Made me day, you have, sir!' chortled Luscombe. 'Driving in a Bentley. Thanks a lot. Esme's going in front, is she?'

He helped her out and shut the door on her after she'd scrambled in. Then he stood waving as they drove off. A nice chap, thought Luscombe. 'E'd do very well for our Miss Julie.

The traffic was heavy; the professor crossed London Bridge and made his slow way south of the river, through Wandsworth, Kingston-upon-Thames and Chertsey, and then picked up speed going through Woking and Guildford, all the while listening to Esme's unceasing chatter, answering her questions with no sign of impatience.

Presently he said over his shoulder, 'There's a rather good pub at Midhurst; I thought we might stop there for lunch. He turned off the main road presently, taking the narrow country roads through charming country, and half an hour later stopped before the Angel Hotel, an old coaching inn skilfully restored.

Esme, peering at it, said, 'I say, this looks splendid and I'm famished.'

'Good. So am I,' said the professor. 'Let us go inside; I'll book a table and take Blotto for a run while you ladies tidy yourselves.'

In the ladies' Esme observed, 'He's sweet, isn't he? And so old-fashioned—I mean, the way he said "tidy yourselves"; anyone else would say going to the loo!'

'I would have felt very uncomfortable if he had said that,' said her mother, 'and I think he knew that. I only hope he's enjoying himself...'

Julie silently hoped the same thing.

They ate in the brasserie—tiny herb pancakes followed by beautifully grilled fish, finishing with creamy concoctions from the sweet trolley while the professor ate cheese and biscuits. Over coffee he said, 'How about going along the coast to Brighton? We can go to Chichester and take the A259 for the rest of the way; it's barely an hour's drive. We'd have plenty of time to go to the pier or wherever you would like to go before tea.'

He smiled round at them, his eyes lingering on Julie's quiet face. She had had little to say and he would have liked to have had her beside him as he drove. He dismissed the thought impatiently. She was encroaching on his well-ordered life; for the second time that day he decided to do something about it.

Strolling with Esme, while Blotto pottered briefly, he was taken by surprise with Esme's question: 'Do you like Julie, Simon?' She peered up at him. 'You always call her Miss Beckworth, don't you? And she doesn't talk about you—only if we ask. Don't you like each other?'

He chose his words carefully. 'Your sister is splendid at her job and a great help to me. We respect each other and that's very important when you work together.'

Esme opened her mouth to say more and closed it again; there had been a steely note in his pleasant voice which she dared not ignore. She said simply, 'She's very clever, you know. I don't mean typing and all that; she cooks almost as well as Luscombe and she sews beautifully. I'd like her to marry someone nice...'

'I'm sure she will; I'm surprised she isn't already married.'

'Well, she's had lots of chances, but she doesn't have much time to go out and, of course, a girl needs lots of pretty clothes to do that.'

The professor, with sisters of his own, agreed with that.

Once through Chichester and on the coast road, he set the car at a good pace, only slowing as they passed through the small seaside towns, so that Hove and Brighton were reached while the afternoon was still young.

They went to the Pavilion first; they inspected the entrance hall, the long gallery, the state apartments and lastly the kitchens. It was here that Julie found herself alone with the professor. Her mother and Esme had wandered off, leaving them in front of a vast row of copper saucepans on one of the walls of the huge place.

'I wonder how many cooks worked here?' said Julie for something to say.

He looked down at her with a faint smile. 'You have been here before?'

'No. It's—well, unusual. Have you?' And before he could reply she added, 'No, of course you haven't; it isn't the sort of place you would take a girl to, is it?'

'Why not?'

'Well, not the kind of girl you take out. I mean—' she was getting flustered '—she'd expect a super restaurant and dancing and black tie and all that. This isn't romantic...'

'Does one need to wear a black tie to be romantic? I would have thought that one could be romantic here in this kitchen if one felt that way inclined.' He

sounded amused. 'Shall we find your mother and
Esme? I dare say we have time to go to the pier.'

They spent half an hour there; Julie and Esme
played the machines, winning small amounts of money
on the fruit machines and losing it again, while her
mother and the professor strolled round. Julie glanced
at them once or twice; they appeared to be getting on
very well. It was impossible to see whether he was
really enjoying himself, though.

They went to the Lanes then, peering into the small
shop windows. There was so much to see: jewellery,
antiques, tiny boutiques with one exquisite garment
flung over a chair in the window, and seaside shops
open still, even though the season was over. They had
tea here, in an olde-worlde tea shoppe, with wait-
resses in mob-caps and dainty little tables ringed with
flimsy chairs. The professor set his large person down
gingerly onto a chair which creaked and groaned under
him.

They ate toasted teacakes and buttered toast and
chocolate eclairs and ordered a second pot of tea.
Julie, passing his cup for the second time, wondered
uneasily just how much their outing was costing him.
She should have refused his offer straight away, she
reflected, and not mentioned her mother and sister;
he had had no choice but to invite them too...

She wondered if he would be more friendly now—
after all, her mother and Esme were on excellent terms
with him, calling him Simon too. She had been careful
not to call him anything for the whole day, and so,
she noticed, had he avoided using her name.

They went back to the car finally and then drove
back to London, reaching it as dusk was turning to
dark, and very much to her surprise he accepted her

mother's offer of coffee. 'I'll take Blotto for a quick run,' he suggested. 'He should be tired out, but five minutes will do him no harm.'

Luscombe was back. 'Thought you might want a bite to eat,' he explained. 'Kettle's on the boil and I've cut some sandwiches. 'Is nibs coming in, is 'e?'

'He's taken Blotto for a quick walk. Luscombe, that's good of you. Have you had your supper? Did you have a good day with your sister?'

'First-rate, Mrs Beckworth. That I should live to see the day I'd ride in a Bentley. Enjoy yourself, did you?'

'Lovely; we went all over the place and saw so much and had a gorgeous lunch. Had we better have coffee in the drawing room?'

'Not on my account, Mrs Beckworth.' The professor had come into the kitchen. He nodded to Luscombe. 'You had a good day too?' he asked.

'I'd say. Best fish and chips in town at my sister's.'

They sat around the table in the warm kitchen, all of them, and Luscombe cut more sandwiches and made more coffee. The talk was cheerful, with Esme and Luscombe doing most of it and Mrs Beckworth putting in a gentle word here and there and the professor joining in from time to time in his quiet voice. As for Julie, she joined in too, trying to ignore the nagging thought that next week she would be back at her desk with the professor in his office. Would this day's outing change things? Perhaps he would be more friendly now; perhaps he would stop calling her Miss Beckworth.

He wasn't there when she arrived on Monday, but there was a note on her desk. 'In path lab if wanted,' with his initials scrawled underneath. Julie opened the post, answered the phone, opened his diary and sat down to start her own work. She had been there for quite some time when the professor walked in, laid some papers on her desk and in an austere voice said, 'Good morning, Miss Beckworth.'

Julie sighed; they were back at square one again. She wished him good morning in a colourless voice, adding a snappy 'sir' and 'Dr MacFinn would like to see you if possible this morning.'

He was standing at her desk, looking at her, which she found unnerving. She poised her hands over her computer and gave him an enquiring look.

'I'll get these notes finished, sir.' She looked away quickly from his thoughtful stare, glad to have an excuse to turn away from his eyes.

CHAPTER FIVE

JULIE saw very little of the professor after that first unsatisfactory conversation. She told herself that she was glad of it—something which she knew wasn't true; she wanted him to like her, to laugh and talk to her as he did with Esme and her mother. She wasn't a conceited girl; she was used to admiring glances and had fended off the tentative advances of several of the young housemen, but the professor's glances were strictly impersonal and he had shown no wish to add warmth to their relationship.

Why should he? she reasoned, when he had a girl waiting for him in Groningen. Or perhaps she wasn't waiting; perhaps they faced a hopeless future with only stolen meetings to keep their love alive. Julie, aware that she was allowing her thoughts to get too romantic, applied herself to her word processor once more.

It was during the morning that a call was put through to her desk.

'I can't contact Professor van der Driesma,' complained the operator. 'I can't get him on his phone. Will you take the call?'

Julie, glad of a diversion, lifted the receiver. The voice was a woman's—a young voice too. 'You are the secretary of Professor van der Driesma? I wish to speak to him, please.'

'He's not here for the moment. Will you hang on and I'll see if I can find him? Who shall I say?'

'Mevrouw van Graaf. I will wait.'

Julie heard the little chuckle as she put down the receiver. 'Drat the man,' said Julie, and went to check the phone on his desk. It hadn't been replaced; no wonder the operator hadn't got his desk. She put it back in its cradle and not very hopefully phoned his bleep. She was surprised when a minute or so later he phoned back.

'I hope it's urgent,' he told her testily before she could speak. 'I'm occupied.'

'Mevrouw van Graaf is on the phone for you, sir.'

He didn't answer at once, then said, 'Ask her for a number, will you? And tell her I'll ring her within half an hour.' He hung up then and she went back to her desk and picked up her own phone.

'Mevrouw van Graaf? The professor can't come to the phone for the moment; he has asked me to get your phone number and he will ring you during the next half-hour.'

'Very well; here is the number. I will wait.' There was a happy little laugh. 'I have waited for a long time and now I do not need to wait. I do not speak of the telephone, you understand...'

'Yes, I understand,' Julie said, and hung up. Something must have happened; Mevrouw van Graaf was free. Free to marry the professor. She didn't want to think about that; it was a good thing that she had so much work on her desk.

He came back presently. 'You have the number?' he asked.

Julie handed him the slip of paper and he went back to his office, leaving the door open. She would have to shut it; she had no intention of eavesdropping although she was longing to know what it was all about. But there was no need to shut the door for he spoke in his own language, although she understood the first word he uttered. *Lieveling*—darling—and an endearment which the Dutch didn't use lightly. Julie tapped away as though her life depended on it, not wishing to hear his voice; even speaking another language it sounded full of delight.

He talked for some time and a glance at the clock showed her that it was time for her to go to her dinner. She didn't like to go in case he needed her for something, so she sat there quietly, listening to the murmur of his voice and his laugh. He rang off presently and came to the open door.

'I have an Outpatients at one o'clock; I'll see you there, Miss Beckworth. There are a couple of tapes for you to type up; they're on my desk.'

'Very well, sir; I'm going to my dinner now.'

He glanced at the clock. 'Yes, yes, of course.' He gave her an absent-minded nod and went away, pausing at the door to say, 'I'm on the ward if I should be wanted. Let them know, will you?'

Julie ate her dinner quickly and hurried back to her desk. Outpatients could sometimes run late and there would be no time for her to type up the tapes as well as the outpatients' notes; she could start on the tapes before one o'clock...

Outpatients was busy, and although it was already running late the professor remained unhurried, giving his full attention to each patient in turn; the nurses came and went for their tea but Sister stayed put at his elbow and so, perforce, did the two students.

Julie filled her notebook with her expert shorthand, sharpened her pencil and longed for her tea. She saw the last patient leave and closed her notebook smartly. It was past five o'clock but if the professor wanted the notes she would have to stay and type them—and the tapes weren't finished . . .

She was roused from her thoughts by his voice. 'Sister, I'm sure you are longing for a cup of tea; would you ring for someone to bring us a tray?' He looked across at Julie. 'And you, Miss Beckworth— it's been a long afternoon?'

She thanked him nicely, thinking that, for her at least, the afternoon wasn't over.

The tea came with a plate of biscuits, and over second cups he said, 'I will drop you off, Miss Beckworth, if you can be ready in half an hour?'

'I thought I'd stay and get these notes typed.'

'No need. I am going to Leeds tomorrow; you will have the day in which to finish any outstanding work.'

There was no point in arguing and Sister was sitting there listening. Julie said, 'Very well, sir,' in a neutral voice and presently went away to get on with the tapes. She didn't get them finished, of course; he had said half an hour and she knew by now that when he said something he meant it. She was ready, her desk tidied, work put away for the morning, when he came back to his office.

He had little to say as he drove her home and what he did say concerned his work and various instructions for her while he was away. He got out when they reached the house, opened her door, waited while she gained the front door, bade her goodnight and got back into his car and drove away.

A most unsatisfactory day, reflected Julie, going into the kitchen to see what Luscombe was cooking for supper.

'You look peaky, Miss Julie; 'ad a rotten day?'

'Yes, Luscombe; all go, if you know what I mean. I wish I could get a job miles away from any hospital, somewhere where people smiled and had time to pass the time of day...'

'Oh, you are low,' said Luscombe. ''Is nibs been tiresome, 'as 'e?'

'Not more than usual. Can I smell macaroni cheese? I'm famished.

'Ten minutes, Miss Julie. Your ma's in the sitting room and Esme's doing her homework.'

Julie went and talked to her mother then, glossing over her unsatisfactory day before helping Esme with her homework, and it wasn't until they were sitting round the table that Mrs Beckworth asked, 'Did Simon say how much he had enjoyed his day out?'

Julie took a mouthful of macaroni cheese. 'He didn't mention it.'

Mrs Beckworth looked surprised. 'Didn't he? How very strange.'

And Esme chimed in, 'But he said he'd had a lovely time. He told me so.'

'He's had a busy day,' said Julie. 'And he's going to Leeds all day tomorrow, he said.'

'Have you quarrelled?' asked Esme.

'Of course not; we're both too busy—we hardly speak unless it's about the work.' Julie spoke so sharply that Esme, ready with more questions, swallowed them instead.

It was Luscombe who voiced his concern the next morning after she had gone to work. 'Miss Julie's got the 'ump,' he observed to Mrs Beckworth. 'Told me she'd like to find another job. It's my 'umble opinion that she and 'is nibs don't suit. On the other hand...'

'They have fallen in love?' suggested Mrs Beckworth.

'And don't know it, of course. 'Is nibs 'as more than likely got a girl already—someone in Holland; so he takes care to be extra stiff, if you see what I mean.'

Mrs Beckworth nodded. 'Yes, yes, Luscombe, but Julie doesn't seem to like him overmuch. When we were out together the other day she hardly spoke to him.'

'Got their lines crossed,' said Luscombe, peeling the potatoes. ''E only 'as to say 'e's got a girl to make it all fair and square and Miss Julie can behave normal-like again. Me, I don't believe she don't like 'im, but she's got her head screwed on straight, 'asn't she? Not the sort to go crazy over a chap when he's already spoken for.'

'It's very worrying,' said Mrs Beckworth.

'It'll all come out in the wash,' said Luscombe.

Julie, laying piles of perfectly typed notes, memoranda and letters on his desk, wished that the professor were there, sitting with his spectacles perched on his nose, ignoring her for the most part and, truth to tell, unaware of her unless he required her services.

He wasn't expected back until the late evening, the head porter, who had a soft spot for her, told Julie when she arrived the next morning. Which meant that she could start on updating the files which Professor Smythe had stashed away in the filing cabinets and which should have gone to the records office long ago. She worked steadily at them all day and, since another hour or so's work on them would have the job done, decided to stay on after five-thirty and finish it.

She phoned home to say that she would be an hour or so late and then settled back to work. There would be no interruptions; the receptionist knew that the professor wasn't in the hospital and no one would phone or come to his office.

She worked steadily; there was more to do than she had expected but since she had started there seemed no point in not finishing. It was quiet in that part of the hospital where the professor had his office, and the sounds of traffic were muffled by the thin fog which had crept over the city. Julie, intent on getting finished, hardly noticed.

Someone opening the professor's door made her turn round. A man stood there, as surprised as she was, although his astonishment turned to a look of cunning that she didn't much care for. She got up and went through the door to the professor's office. 'You're visiting someone in the hospital?' she asked, and hoped that her voice wasn't wobbling too much. 'You've got lost—you need to go back along the passage and go up the stairs to the wards.'

The man laughed. 'Me? I'm not lost. You just sit quiet, like a good girl, and no one will hurt you.' He went past her and picked up her handbag from the desk.

'What do you think you are doing?' asked Julie angrily. 'Put that down at once. Get out of here...' She picked up the phone and had it snatched from her before she could utter a word into it. 'Now, now, that won't do. I told you to be good, didn't I?' He pushed her into the chair opposite the desk. 'You sit quiet or else...'

He began opening drawers in the professor's desk, sweeping papers onto the floor, pocketing some loose change lying there, and the Waterman pen that the professor used. There was a silver-framed photo in one of the drawers—Julie had never seen it before. He smashed the glass, threw the photo onto the desk and put the frame into his pocket. She could see that it was of a young woman and just for a moment she forgot her fright—so the professor kept a photo of his future wife tucked away in his desk like any lovesick young man. She smiled at the thought and then went white as the man came round the desk to her, grinning.

'Easy as kiss me hand,' he boasted. 'Walk in, I did, just like that, and that old codger in his little box doing his crossword didn't even see me. Now you'll tell me where there's some cash and, better still, I'll wait here while you fetch it.'

'I haven't the least idea where there's any money,' said Julie in a voice which didn't sound quite like hers. 'The cleaners will be along in a minute to collect the waste paper and turn off the lights. You're a fool to think you can get away with this. What are you doing here, anyway?'

'Thought I'd have a look around; didn't know I'd find a pretty girl—what yer doing with all this junk?' His eye roved over the computer and the answering machine, and he picked up the heavy paperweight on the desk. 'Let's smash 'em up...'

Julie's fright turned to rage; she darted from the chair that he had made her sit in, picked up the inkstand on the desk—a Victorian monstrosity of size and weight—and flung it at the man. Her aim was poor; it sailed past him and narrowly missed the professor as he opened the door, whistling past his ear to crash in the passage beyond.

The professor, not a swearing man, was surprised into uttering an oath of some richness—a welcome sound to Julie, doing her best to evade the man's clutches. 'Oh, hurry up, do!' she shouted. 'This fool's tearing the place to pieces.'

A needless remark as it turned out, for the professor had picked the man up by his coat collar and flung him into the chair that she had just left.

'Stay there,' he said in a flinty voice, and reached for the phone. As he dialed he glanced at Julie. 'You're all right, Miss Beckworth?'

She glared at him, conscious of enormous relief at the sight of him and at the same time furious with him for taking it for granted that she was all right. Of course she wasn't; she wanted to scream, indulge in a burst of tears and be cosseted with a cup of tea and a few kind words.

She said in a small voice stiff with dignity, 'Thank you, Professor, I am perfectly all right.'

He nodded at her, spoke into the phone and then sat her down in his chair, turning his attention to the man.

'Exactly why are you here?' he wanted to know. 'And how dare you frighten my secretary and make havoc of my office. I've called the police.'

The man peered up at him. 'Look, guv, I didn't mean no 'arm. Thought I'd find something to nick— it's easy to get into this place. Cor, I could've been in any of the wards but I thought I'd 'ave a peek round first . . .'

'Are you a thief by trade?' asked the professor. 'Or is this a one-off thing?'

The man looked sly. 'That's telling. Now, if you was to let me go... I 'aven't done no 'arm, only knocked a few things around...'

The professor's eyes studied the papers scattered on the floor and Julie's handbag flung onto the desk, its contents scattered too. He looked at Julie then, although he didn't say anything; only when the man started to get up did he say quietly, 'I shouldn't start anything if I were you; I shall knock you down.'

He was lounging against his desk, quite at his ease, and the three of them remained silent until presently there was the reassuring sound of the deliberate footsteps of the two police officers who came in. The elder man took one look at the man and said, 'Slim Sid. Up to your tricks again, are you?' He turned to the professor. 'Now, sir, if you will tell me what he's been up to.'

Two porters had followed the officers into the office. The professor sent them away and closed the door. 'I think Miss Beckworth can give you a better account than I, Officer. I—er—didn't get here until this man—Sid—had had time to cause this havoc. Miss Beckworth was coping with the situation with some spirit; she will tell you what occurred.'

He looked at Julie then and smiled; she hadn't known that a smile could wrap you round, make you feel safe and cherished and, despite the regrettable circumstances, happy. She sat up straight and gave a clear account of what had happened, and even if her voice was somewhat higher than usual and still a little wobbly she added no embellishments. When she had finished she added, 'I shouldn't have thrown the inkstand...'

The elder officer said comfortably, 'No, miss, but, in the circumstances, an understandable action—and you did miss him.'

Julie caught the professor's eye. She had very nearly hit him, hadn't she? Supposing she had? She might have killed him; the inkstand was as heavy as lead—perhaps it *was* lead; it would have bashed his head in...

She drew a sharp breath, feeling sick at the thought. To have ended his life like that... Her life would have ended too; she wouldn't have wanted to go on living without him.

This was neither the time nor the place to discover that she loved him; indeed, she couldn't have discovered it at a more inconvenient time, but there it was... She looked away from him quickly, thankful that the younger officer was asking her for her name and address.

'Just routine, miss,' he added soothingly. 'Slim Sid here is wanted for two break-ins already; since he's stolen nothing here it'll be taken into account but I doubt if he'll be charged.'

They went away presently with Sid, suitably handcuffed, between them. The professor went into the passage, picked up the inkstand, put it back on the desk and lifted the telephone, asking for tea to be brought to his office, and then stood looking at Julie.

'That was a warm welcome you gave me,' he observed mildly.

She burst into tears.

He sat down in the other chair, saying nothing while she sniffed and snorted, and when the tea came he took the tray from the porter and poured out a cup, put it in front of her on the desk and put a large, snowy handkerchief into her hand. 'Mop up,' he bade her, and he spoke very kindly. 'There's nothing like a good cry—much better than bottling it up. Drink your tea and tell me what happened. I only wish I had been here to prevent you being frightened like that.'

Julie gave a prodigious sniff. 'I nearly killed you...'

He took his sopping handkerchief from her. 'No, no, I'm made of sterner stuff. I must admit that I was taken aback.'

He had come to sit on the desk close to her chair; now he put a cup in her hand. 'Drink up and tell me exactly what happened.'

The tea was hot and sweet and very strong. 'I must look awful,' said Julie.

He studied her tear-stained face, the faint pink of her delightful nose, the puffy eyelids, her neat head of hair no longer all that neat.

'You look beautiful,' he told her.

She choked on her tea. He didn't mean it of course; he was saying that to make her feel better.

The professor watched her without appearing to do so. She had probably thought him an unfeeling monster for not offering instant sympathy when he had come into his office, but if he had she would have wept all over him—something she would have regretted later on; she hadn't shown weakness or fear of the intruder; to have burst into tears in front of him would have been something that she would have regretted afterwards. He had put her on her mettle and her report to the police had been sensible and clear.

She finished her tea, thanked him politely for it and collected the contents of her handbag. 'I'll just get these papers cleared up—I hadn't quite finished, I'm afraid.' She peeped at him. 'They're in a great muddle, I'm afraid.'

'They can stay as they are. I'll lock the door and tell the porter that no one is to come in. They can be seen to in the morning.'

'You have a ward-round at eleven o'clock, sir.'

'Plenty of time before then,' he said comfortably. He picked up the phone and dialled a number. She turned sharply to look at him in surprise when he said, 'Mrs Beckworth? We have been delayed here—an unexpected upheaval. No, no, Julie's quite all right. I'm taking her back with me to have a meal and a rest; I'll drive her back later.'

He listened for a few moments. 'In a couple of hours, Mrs Beckworth,' he said, and then put the receiver down.

Julie was staring at him. 'We'll go and have a meal and I will drive you home presently.'

'There's no need. Really, just because I made a fool of myself, crying like a baby. If you don't mind I'll stay and clear up some of this mess and then go home.'

'I do mind. Get your jacket and we'll go.'

'Where?' asked Julie.

'My home. My manservant will have something ready; he expected me back this evening.' When she hesitated he said, 'I've driven down from Leeds and I've had a busy day. I'm hungry.'

There wasn't much point in arguing with him, and besides, she was hungry too. It was a friendly gesture on his part—the kind of gesture anyone might make in like circumstances. Probably he would be bored with her company even for a brief hour or so, but she would see where he lived, perhaps discover something of his life; he might even tell her about the girl that he had met in Groningen. If she knew when he was going to get married it might be easier to forget that she had fallen in love with him.

She had a lot to think about, she reflected, going with him to the car.

The streets were quieter now that the rush hour was over, the evening traffic not yet busy; he drove across the city and she saw presently that they were going through quiet streets of dignified houses with enclosed gardens and, here and there, trees.

The professor turned down a narrow lane beside a terrace of Regency houses and turned into the mews behind them. The cottages in it were charming, with flower boxes at their windows and pristine paintwork. He drove to the end and stopped outside the last cottage, got out and opened her door to usher her into a small lobby with a glass inner door.

This was opened as they went in by a middle-aged man, very dignified. He bade them good evening in a grave voice and the professor said, 'This is Blossom, who runs the place for me. Blossom, this is Miss Beckworth, whom I have brought home for a meal— she's had a rather trying experience at the hospital this evening.'

'Indeed, miss, I am sorry to hear it. There is a fire in the sitting room, sir. A glass of sherry, perhaps, for the young lady while I dish up?'

Her jacket tenderly borne away by Blossom, Julie was ushered into the sitting room which ran from the front of the cottage to the back, with windows at each end and a fireplace opposite the door. It was low-ceilinged, its walls hung with honey-coloured paper, and furnished with cosy armchairs, a lovely old corner-cupboard, a satinwood rent table under one window and small lamp-tables here and there. The lamps on them had been lighted and gave the room a most welcoming look.

'Come and sit by the fire,' suggested the professor, and pulled forward a chair covered in mulberry velvet, 'and take Blossom's advice.'

He went to a small table to pour the drinks. 'Dry, or something sweeter?'

'Dry, please.' Her eyes had lighted on a basket to one side of the fireplace. 'Oh, you have a cat...'

'Yes, and kittens; there should be two there.'

Julie got up to look. The cat opened an eye and studied her before closing it again, and she bent nearer. Two very small kittens were tucked between her paws.

'She's called Kitty—not very imaginative, I'm afraid, but Blossom assures me that she replies to that name.'

Julie sat down again and took the glass he offered. 'And the kittens?'

'They arrived shortly after she attached herself to us. A boy and a girl. I've had several offers of homes for them but I fancy that by the time they are old enough to leave their mother Blossom will refuse to part with them.'

He had gone to sit down opposite her and bent to stroke the cat. 'I must admit it is pleasant to come home to a welcome.'

'You miss Jason...'

'Indeed I do. I shall be going to Holland shortly and hope to spend a few days with him.' He smiled. 'A holiday this time.'

Julie said in a steady voice, 'I am sure you will enjoy that; you must miss your family and friends.'

'I have friends here as well.' An unsatisfactory answer, almost a snub. Justified, she reflected fairly; his private life was no concern of hers.

She sipped her sherry and racked her brains for something to say. Luckily Blossom came to tell them that dinner was served and they crossed the little hall to a small dining room at the front of the cottage. It held a round table encircled by six Hepplewhite chairs, and there was a small sideboard and a long-case clock, its front of marquetry. The table, covered in white damask, was set with silver and crystal glasses and the plates were delft china. Did the professor dine in such state each evening? she wondered, sampling the soup set before her. Tomato and orange—home-made, too.

The professor seemed determined to keep on friendly terms, and indeed he was a perfect host, talking about this and that as they ate their duckling with cherry sauce and game chips, never mentioning the evening's unfortunate event as he invited her to have a second helping of Blossom's delicious hot almond fritters. Only when they were once more in the sitting room drinking their coffee did he ask her if she felt quite recovered. 'If you wish there is no reason why you shouldn't have a day at home tomorrow.'

She thought of the mess in his office. 'I'm quite all right, really I am,' she told him. 'I'm ashamed of myself for being such a baby.'

'My dear girl, you behaved with exemplary calm; most women would have screeched the house down.'

'I was too scared to scream,' she told him.

'In future if you are working late you are to lock the door. You understand me, Miss Beckworth?' He sounded chillingly polite; the little flame of hope that he had decided to like her after all died. He had done his duty as he saw it; now she was Miss Beckworth again. It was ridiculous to imagine that she could possibly marry such a man; she put down her cup and saucer and observed in a voice devoid of expression that she would like to go home.

'It has been most kind of you,' said Julie, in a voice which sounded in her own ears to be far too gushing. The professor must have thought the same, for he glanced at her in faint surprise. 'I hope I haven't interrupted your evening.'

'No, no. I had nothing planned. I'll drive you home.'

They went into the hall and Blossom appeared, soft-footed and silent. 'I enjoyed dinner very much,' she told him. 'I wish I could cook like that; thank you, Blossom.'

He smiled then. 'A pleasure, Miss Beckworth. I trust you have fully recovered from your unpleasant experience?'

'Yes, thank you. Goodnight.'

The professor had stood by while she had talked; now he ushered her out to the car, got in beside her, and drove away, back through the city, away from the quiet streets and the gardens and trees until he turned into the gate of her home.

Julie made to get out, embarking on a rather muddled speech of thanks to which he didn't listen but got out and opened her door and walked with her to the door of the house. Here she held out a hand.

'You've been most kind,' she began once again. 'Please don't wait—'

'I'm coming in,' said the professor.

The door was opened by Luscombe. 'There yer are, Miss Julie; come on in, both of you. Evening to you, Professor. Here's a turn-up for the book, eh?'

He closed the door behind them as Mrs Beckworth came out of the sitting room.

'Darling, whatever has happened? You're all right? Oh, of course you are; the professor's with you. Did you faint or feel ill? Come in and tell us what happened.'

Julie took off her jacket and they went into the sitting room to where Esme was sitting in her dressing gown with Blotto sprawled on her lap. She jumped up as they went in. 'I wouldn't go to bed until you came home, Julie; Simon, do tell us what happened.'

Julie went to pat Blotto and her mother waved the professor to a chair. Luscombe had followed them in and was standing by the door, all ears.

'Your sister was working late when a man got into the hospital and found his way to my office. He flung things around and threatened her. She was very brave; she threw an inkstand at him—'

'You hit him, Julie?' asked Esme, all agog.

'Well, no, and it only just missed the professor as he came into the room.'

'My dear Simon, you weren't hurt?' asked Mrs Beckworth anxiously.

'I? Not at all. I was lost in admiration for your daughter's presence of mind in throwing something at the man; it put him off his stroke completely.'

'Then what did you do?' asked Esme.

'The police came and took the man away; it seems he was known to them. We had a cup of tea and then a meal. You have a daughter to be proud of, Mrs Beckworth.'

Julie looked at her feet and Mrs Beckworth said, 'Thank you for looking after her so well, Simon. We're so grateful. Would you like a cup of coffee?'

'I won't stay, Mrs Beckworth, thank you; but I felt it necessary to explain what happened. Rest assured I'm going to make sure that it can never happen again.'

He bade them all goodnight, adding to Julie, 'Don't come in in the morning if you don't feel up to it.'

She mumbled an answer, not looking at him. Just because she had been silly and cried, there was no excuse to take a day off.

When he had gone Mrs Beckworth said, 'Now, darling, do tell us again what happened. I mean before Simon arrived. Was the man very nasty? He didn't hurt you?'

'No, but he flung things about—all the notes and files and case-sheets on the desk; he threw them all onto the floor. It'll take all day to get them straight. He wanted to break up the computer too. I couldn't reach the phone...'

'You were very brave, throwing something at him.'

'You always were a rotten shot,' said Esme. 'A good thing too; you might have knocked out Simon and I'd never have forgiven you.'

I wouldn't have forgiven myself either, reflected Julie.

Luscombe came in then, with a tray of tea. 'Nothing like a cuppa when you've 'ad a bit of a set-to,' he pointed out. He chuckled. 'I'd have liked to have seen the professor's face when he opened the door... I bet 'e was livid.'

Thinking about it, Julie realised that he had been very angry. Not noisily so; it had been a cold, fierce rage. No wonder the man hadn't attempted to get out of the chair that he had been thrown into. She hoped that the professor would never look at her like that.

Julie went to work early the next morning, intent on clearing up the mess before he got there, but early though she was he was earlier, crouched down on the floor, sorting out the scattered sheets.

'Oh, you're here already,' said Julie, and then added, 'Good morning, sir.'

He glanced up. 'Good morning, Miss Beckworth. What a very thorough job Slim Sid did. I am afraid he has torn several pages of notes. However, let us first of all get everything sorted out.'

He handed her a pile of folders, observing mildly, 'The floor is the best place.'

So she got on her knees and went to work. It was dull and tedious, and since he showed no signs of wanting to talk she kept silent. Before long the phone rang, and when she answered it it was an urgent request that he should go at once to the wards. Which left her alone with her thoughts.

CHAPTER SIX

BY THE time the professor came back Julie had established some kind of order. There had been a good deal of sorting out to do and her normal day's work was already piled on her desk. She had paused briefly to open the post and lay the contents on his desk, find his diary and leave it open—it was crammed with appointments—and had dealt with several phone calls which hadn't been urgent.

He went past her into his own office without speaking and presently asked her to take some letters. As she sat down he looked at her over his spectacles. 'You are suffering no ill effects from your disturbed evening?' he wanted to know.

'None, sir.' She opened her notebook, pencil poised. After a quick look she bent her head, writing the date on her pad, taking her time over it, wishing that he would start dictating, because sitting there with him was a mixed blessing; it was pure happiness to be near him; on the other hand, the sooner he started dictating with his usual abruptness, apparently unaware of her as a person, the easier it would be for her to ignore her feelings.

The professor was, however, in no hurry. He was irritated that Julie was so frequently in his thoughts and yesterday he had, much against his will, told her that she was beautiful and been altogether too concerned about her. He had been so careful to hold her at arm's length when it was obvious that she didn't like him. Hopefully, she had been so upset that she had probably not been listening. He would have to be careful; he had no intention of allowing himself to fall in love with a girl who so disliked him.

He thought with relief of the few days' holiday he intended to take in Holland; to get away might bring him to his senses so that he could return to his austere, hard-working life.

He pushed his spectacles further up his handsome nose. 'The hospital director—you have his name and the hospital's in the letter—Stockholm. With regard to your invitation to lecture...'

Would he want her to go to Stockholm with him? Julie wondered, her pencil racing over the page. Perhaps not for such a brief visit to read a paper at a seminar there. She turned the page for a new letter and concentrated; this time it was full of long medical terms—she would have to check it all in her dictionary.

He went away presently and she made a cup of coffee before starting on her typing—the letters first and then printing out the spoilt sheets again and then getting down to the routine paperwork. The professor was still absent and she decided that she would miss her dinner. If there was a porter free he might bring her a sandwich from the canteen.

She rang through to the lodge, and since she was regarded as something of a heroine after last night's escapade a few minutes later one of the porters who had followed the police brought her a plate of sandwiches. 'Beef, miss, and a packet of biscuits. All right for coffee, are you?' When she thanked him, he said awkwardly, 'Wish I'd known about that fellow getting in here; I'd have put him to the right about. None the worse are you, miss?'

She assured him that she had never felt better. 'And I know you would have been the first to deal with him. I feel quite safe here. It was just chance that he managed to creep in.'

The professor returned just as she had taken a bite of sandwich. He eyed her coldly. 'Why have you not gone to your dinner, Miss Beckworth? Am I such a hard taskmaster?'

She said thickly through a mouthful of beef, 'No, no, sir, but the work's piling up and there's a lot of time wasted in the canteen, queueing for food.'

He looked surprised and then picked up the phone and asked for sandwiches and coffee to be sent to his office. Julie swallowed the last of the beef; it seemed that he was going to lunch at his desk too...

She was wrong; the porter, when he came with a tray bearing a pot of coffee and sandwiches, was directed to put them on her desk, and when she turned a surprised face to him Professor van der Driesma said, 'They were for you, Miss Beckworth.'

The professor came through the door as the porter went away. Julie eyed the sandwiches with pleasure—egg and cress, ham, and a couple of leaves of lettuce on the side—very tasty. She said gratefully, 'Thank you, sir.'

He paused on his way out. 'I cannot allow you to waste away, Miss Beckworth.'

Her 'Well, really!' was lost on him as he closed the door gently behind him.

She drank a cup of delicious coffee and ate the sandwiches. What had he meant? Had it been an oblique reference to her size? She was a big girl but she had a splendid shape. Perhaps he preferred the beanpole type—or did he think that she was greedy?

She ate another sandwich. 'Well, too bad!' said Julie, gobbling the last delicious morsel and pouring the last of the coffee. Though the canteen, if they knew that she was lunching off what was intended to be a light snack for a consultant, would be furious.

She started her work again, much refreshed, and by the time the professor came back, his head bent over the papers before him, she had finished her work. She took his letters in, waited to see if he needed her for anything else and went back to her office to start on the filing.

He had given her the briefest of glances and returned to his work again. I might just as well not be here, she reflected. Why does it all have to be so hopeless? Why couldn't he have fallen in love with me? And why did I have to fall in love with him? Useless questions she couldn't answer. She finished her filing, bade him a wooden goodnight and took herself off home.

Luscombe was in the kitchen when she went in. ''Arf a mo', there's a cup of tea coming up,' he told her. ''Ad a bad day?'

'Absolutely beastly.' She drank her tea and felt better, so she was able to tell her mother that she wasn't in the least tired and the day had been no busier than usual.

'Well, dear, that's a good thing. Do you remember Peter Mortimer? He went to Australia—or was it New Zealand?—last year. He's back home and phoned to see if you'd have dinner with him this evening. You used to be quite friendly...' Her mother looked hopeful. 'He said he'd ring again.'

Which he did, exactly on cue. 'Remember me?' he asked cheerfully. 'I'm here in town for a couple of days before I go home. Will you have dinner with me this evening and tell me all the gossip?'

She had liked him and he had more than liked her, but she had almost forgotten what he looked like. He sounded lonely and perhaps an evening out would restore her spirits. After all, what was the use of mooning over a man who hardly looked at her, much less bothered to say anything other than good morning and good evening? 'I'd like that,' she told him. 'Do you want me to meet you somewhere?'

'I'll come for you. Seven o'clock be too early?'

'That's fine.' She ran off and went to tell her mother.

'How nice, dear. You have so little fun these days. I wonder where he'll take you?'

'No idea.' To discourage her mother's obvious hopes, she added, 'He's in town just for a day or two then he's going home.'

She put on a pretty silk jersey dress, its colour matching her hair, piled her hair in a complicated topknot and went to her mother's wardrobe to get the coat—a dark brown cashmere treasured from their better-off days and shared between them, used only on special occasions.

Esme was in the sitting room when she went downstairs. 'You look quite chic,' she observed. 'Take care of the coat, won't you? In a year or two I'll be able to borrow it too.'

'Such a useful garment,' said Mrs Beckworth. 'I shall need it for that committee meeting in a couple of days' time. You know the one—we drink weak tea and decide about the Christmas party for the rest home. Only they're all so dressy. I know I've worn the coat for several years, but no one can cavil at cashmere, can they?' She paused. 'There's the doorbell. You go, dear; Luscombe's busy in the kitchen.'

Peter Mortimer hadn't changed; he had a round, chubby face and bright blue eyes and no one took him seriously, although he was something successful in the advertising business. He came in and spent five minutes talking to Mrs Beckworth. Esme bombarded him with questions about Australia—only it turned out that it was New Zealand—but presently he suggested that they should go. 'I've got a table for eight o'clock and we're bound to get hung up crossing town.'

He was an easy companion, delighted to talk about his year away from England, and Julie was a good listener. The traffic was heavy but he was a good driver and patient. 'Not boring you?' he asked as he drew up outside the Café Royal. 'Pop inside while I get this chappie to park the car...'

Julie went into the foyer, left the coat in the cloakroom and hoped that he wouldn't be too long. He wasn't. 'Marvellous chap—tucked the car somewhere. Hope this place suits you?'

'Peter, it's heavenly. I haven't been out to dine for months.'

They were shown to their table and when they had sat down he asked, 'Why not?' He grinned. 'A gorgeous girl like you? I should have thought you'd have been out night after night, if not spoken for!'

'Well, I'm not. I know it sounds silly but I'm quite tired when I get home in the evenings and there's always something which has to be done. Don't think

I'm grumbling; I've a good job and lots of friends, only I don't see any of them as often as I'd like to.' She looked around her at the opulent grill room with its gilded rococo and mirrors. 'This is quite something. Are you a millionaire or something?'

'Lord, no, but I'm doing quite nicely. I'm going back to New Zealand in a couple of weeks. Came over to see the parents, actually.' He looked suddenly bashful. 'I'm going to marry a girl—her father's a sheep farmer on the South Island; thought I'd better tell them about her. We'll marry after Christmas and come over here to see them.'

'Peter, how lovely! I hope you'll be very happy. Tell me about her...'

'Let's have a drink and decide what we'll eat—I've some photos of her...'

They had their drinks and decided what they would have—spinach soufflé, medallions of pork with ginger sauce—and, since Peter insisted that it was a kind of celebration—or a reunion if she'd rather—he ordered a bottle of champagne.

The soufflé eaten, he brought out the photos and they bent over them, their heads close together. 'She looks very pretty, Peter; she's dark, and her eyes are lovely.' Julie sat back while the waiter served her, and glanced round the room. The professor was sitting thirty yards away, staring at her.

He wasn't alone; the woman he was with had her back to Julie, but, from what she could see of it, it promised elegance. She had dark hair, cut short, a graceful neck and shoulders and when she turned her head, a perfect profile.

Julie managed a small, social smile and looked away quickly, not wanting to see if he would acknowledge it or not. Probably not, she thought peevishly, bending an apparently attentive head to hear Peter's description of life in New Zealand.

Who was the woman? she wondered. Of course, the professor was entitled to have as many girlfriends as he wanted, but what about the girl in Groningen? There had been no mistaking the way he had held her close and kissed her.

She had never thought of him as having a social life; to see him, sitting there in black tie, in one of the most fashionable restaurants in London, had surprised her. Just for a moment she wondered if he would say anything to her in the morning, but she dismissed the thought as Peter began a detailed description of the house he intended to buy for his bride.

When she contrived to peep towards the professor's table later it was to find that he and his companion had gone.

In the morning the professor was already at his desk when she got to her office. His good morning was affable. 'You had a pleasant evening, Miss Beckworth?' He sounded positively avuncular.

'Thank you, yes, very pleasant. Shall I ring the path lab for those results they promised for this morning?'

He didn't answer this. 'An old friend?' he asked.

'Oh, yes,' said Julie briskly. 'We've known each other for a very long time.' She wasn't sure how one simpered but it seemed an appropriate expression and she did her best.

The professor watched with secret amusement. 'I suppose we shall be losing you shortly,' he suggested. 'He didn't look the kind of man who would like his wife to work.'

Julie was thinking about the woman at the professor's table and wasn't listening with more than half an ear. 'He still has to get his house—of course, in that part of New Zealand there is plenty of space.'

'New Zealand? That's a long way away.'

'Twenty-four hours in a plane,' she told him, and added briskly, 'I'll phone the path lab...'

He watched her go to her office and pick up the phone, surprised to find that he didn't like the idea of her going to the other side of the world as another man's wife.

He gave an impatient sigh; she had somehow wormed her way into his mind and now his heart, and, what was worse, she was quite unaware of it. Well, he would never let her see that; a pity that after all these years he should be in danger of falling in love at last, and with the wrong girl. He opened his diary and studied its contents; a busy day lay ahead of him. He was too old for her, anyway.

That evening when he got home Blossom came to meet him. 'Mrs Venton telephoned, sir, not half an hour ago. Asked if you would ring her back. I did tell her that I didn't know how late you'd be.'

The professor paused on his way to his study. 'Ah, thank you, Blossom. Did she say why she wished me to ring her?'

'She mentioned a small dinner party with a few friends, sir.' Blossom coughed. 'The young lady whom you brought here recently, sir—I trust she is fully recovered from her nasty experience? I had the whole story from your head porter's wife while shopping at the supermarket.'

'Quite recovered, Blossom.'

'I am glad to hear it; a very nice young lady if I may say so, sir, and extremely pretty. Very well liked, I understand.' He slid past the professor and opened his study door for him. 'I lighted a small fire, sir; these evenings are chilly. Will you dine at your usual time?'

'Please.'

The professor went and sat at his desk, ignoring the papers on it, so still that Kitty in her basket by the fire left her sleeping kittens and climbed onto his knee. He stroked her gently while he thought about Julie. Despite her evasive answers to his questions he felt sure now that the man she had been with was no more than a friend. From where he had been sitting he had had an excellent view of the pair of them; they certainly hadn't behaved like people in love and yet he had had the distinct impression that that was what she would have liked him to think.

Since he was now quite certain in his mind that he loved her and intended, by hook or crook to marry her, he would have to find ways of getting to know her better, and that, he knew, would have to be a gradual process or she would be frightened off. First he must win her liking.

Blossom, coming to tell him that dinner was ready, wondered why he looked so thoughtful and at the same time so cheerful. Surely that Mrs Venton hadn't had that effect upon his master. A tiresome woman, thought Blossom, out to catch the professor, given the chance. Not that he would be an easy man to catch, but sooner or later someone would do just that.

Blossom, serving soup with the same perfection he would have shown at a dinner party for a dozen, thought of Julie again. She would do nicely.

It would have given him great peace of mind if he had known that the professor had come to the same conclusion, never mind his previous doubts.

Julie, unaware of these plans for her future, her feelings ruffled because the professor had shown no emotion when she had hinted that she might be going to New Zealand, went home in a bad temper, didn't eat her supper and flounced around the house doing a lot of unnecessary things like shaking up the cushions and opening and closing drawers and cupboards.

Her mother, placidly sewing name-tapes on Esme's new sports kit, watched her and said nothing; only later, when Julie had taken herself off to bed, did she remark to Luscombe worriedly, 'Julie doesn't seem quite herself. I do hope she's not sickening for something.'

Luscombe offered the warm drink he had thoughtfully prepared for her.

'In love, isn't she? I said so, didn't I? 'Ad a row, no doubt, with the professor...'

'When he's here he hardly speaks to her. I mean, she's his secretary.' A muddled statement which Luscombe had no difficulty in understanding.

'Goes to show—'e's smitten too. The pair of them 'as got crossed wires.'

On Monday the professor began his campaign to win Julie's attention, if not her affection, with caution. Nevertheless, she looked at him once or twice during the day; he had smiled at her several times, he had wished her a cheerful good morning and each time he came and went to and from his office he had a word to say; she could only conclude that he had had some good news of some sort. Perhaps that girl was coming to see him. He had told her that he would be going back to Holland shortly—the prospect of being at his home again might have put him in a good mood. She responded guardedly, carefully polite.

The professor, sitting at his desk watching Julie's charming back view as she typed, abandoned the notes he was preparing for a lecture and reviewed the situation; after three days there had been no obvious signs of Julie responding to his overtures of friendship. On the contrary, she was, if anything, decidedly tart. A lesser man might have been warned off, but the professor was made of sterner stuff. He brought his powerful brain to bear on the problem and reflected that he was enjoying himself.

The next day he told Julie that he would be going to Holland that evening. 'A few days' holiday,' he told her airily, 'and most conveniently Dr Walter's secretary is off sick, so you will be standing in for her. Perhaps you will look in here each morning and check through the post.'

Julie put the folder of papers down on his desk. However would she get through the days without him? To see his empty desk each morning and wonder what he was doing and with whom... 'How long will you be gone, sir?' she asked him.

He glanced up at her. 'A week—ten days. I'm not sure. I intend to see something of my family and friends and I want to spend a few days at least at my home. It rather depends on circumstances. George Wyatt—his registrar—will deal with anything which may crop up.'

'Very well, sir. If you should see Mevrouw Schatt give her my kind regards.'

'Of course.' He turned briskly to his desk. 'I see that in my diary you have a note reminding me to phone Mrs Venton. Perhaps you would be good enough to do that for me and tell her that I shall be away for the next week or so.'

'Very well. Is she the lady you were dining with at the Café Royal?'

He stared at her and she couldn't read the expression on his face.

'Since you ask—yes, Miss Beckworth.' He opened his eyes wide. 'Why do you ask?'

'Because I'm a nosy parker!' said Julie flippantly, and picked up the phone as it started to ring.

She rang Mrs Venton while he was on the wards and relayed his message in an impersonal voice.

'Who are you?' asked Mrs Venton rudely.

'Professor van der Driesma's secretary.'

'Where has he gone? You must know that. And when is he coming back?'

'I have no idea when he will be returning, Mrs Venton, and I have given you his message exactly as he gave it to me.'

'He's there now, isn't he?' Mrs Venton wasn't going to give up.

'No, Mrs Venton, he isn't here.'

'I don't believe you,' snapped Mrs Venton, and slammed down the receiver.

In an expressionless voice Julie reported the conversation when the professor returned. It was most unsatisfactory that all he did was grunt.

At five o'clock he looked up from his computer.
'That will be all for today, Miss Beckworth. Good
evening.'

She tidied her desk and wished him goodbye and
a pleasant holiday.

That night she had a good cry, thinking of him on
his way to Holland. He'll probably come back
married, she thought miserably. It was easy to account for his friendly manner now, he must have been
happy...

The professor wasn't exactly happy, he realised that
he would never be quite happy again unless he had
Julie for his wife, but he was pleased enough with his
careful planning. Absence makes the heart grow
fonder, he reminded himself as he drove down to
Dover, and if he wasn't distracted by the sight of
Julie's beautiful face each day, he would be able to
mull over the more likely schemes he had in mind.

It was very late by the time he reached his home in
Leiden, but Siska and Jason gave him a warm
welcome. He ate his supper while she told him all the
latest news, took a delighted Jason for a walk and
went to his bed, where he slept the dreamless sleep of
a man who knew what he wanted to do and would
do it.

To Mrs Beckworth's bright enquiry as to how the
professor did, Julie, when she got home, replied
briefly that she didn't know because he had gone away.

'Not for good?' Mrs Beckworth asked in a dismayed voice.

'No, no. He's going to Holland this evening for a holiday; he doesn't know how long he'll be away. I've been loaned to Dr Walters—his secretary's ill.'

'Oh, well, that will make a nice change, darling. Is he nice, this other doctor?'

'He's a medical consultant. He's all right in a dull kind of way.'

A not very satisfactory answer, thought her mother. 'Let's hope Simon has a nice break. I'm sure he deserves one.'

Julie mumbled a reply and went off to help Esme with her maths.

Dr Walters was pleased to see her in the morning. Miss Frisby, his own secretary, he explained, hadn't been feeling well for some days—something to do with her teeth. 'I'm afraid the filing and so forth has got rather neglected—she didn't feel up to it.'

Discovering the havoc in the filing cabinets, Julie concluded that Miss Frisby couldn't have been feeling up to it for weeks—even months. The muddle would keep her busy for hours, not to mention the routine work that she was expected to do as well. Perhaps if her teeth didn't improve Miss Frisby would resign. Julie knew her by sight—a washed-out girl with straggly hair and a loud and refined voice—but they had never said more than hello. They weren't likely to.

The post piled up on the professor's desk, and she quickly decided that she would have to go in to work an hour earlier each morning, so her days were busy. When she got home in the evening there was always plenty to keep her occupied—Esme to help with her homework, her mother to talk to and Luscombe to help around the house. Despite all this, the days dragged.

The professor had been gone for several days when Esme received a postcard from him. It was from Leiden, showing a view of the Rappenburg. He had written in his almost unreadable scrawl: 'I'll show you this one day. Ask your sister if she remembers it.'

Esme, proudly handing it round, said reflectively, 'He never calls you Julie, does he? Do you call him Simon?'

'Certainly not.' Julie hadn't meant to sound snappy, and she added quickly, 'That would never do—he's rather an important person at the hospital.'

Esme persisted. 'Yes, but when you're alone with him?'

'He's still my boss.'

'I wonder what he's doing?' mused Esme.

Julie wondered too, but she didn't say so.

Simon was sitting at the head of his table in the rather gloomy dining room of Huis Driesma. A large square house, its exterior belying its interior, redolent of a bygone age, it stood in grounds bordered by water meadows on a lake fringed by trees and shrubs, fronting a narrow country road. Out of sight round a bend in the road was a small village, its cottages petering out as it wound away into a tranquil distance.

There were a number of people seated at the table: Simon's mother faced him at its foot, then his two brothers and their wives, and his youngest brother, still a medical student, sat beside the youngest of all of them—a girl of almost seventeen.

The conversation had been animated, for although they were a close family they lived at some distance from each other, and for them all to be together was seldom possible. The house was Simon's, inherited from his father, and until he should marry his mother lived there with his sister and—whenever he could get away from the hospital—his younger brother, Hugo.

His mother was saying now, 'I wish you would marry, Simon; it is time you took over this house. I know you have a charming house in Leiden, but you should spend more time here. Weekends, perhaps? I know you have your work at St Bravo's, but travelling is so easy these days...'

Celeste, the baby of the family, chimed in. 'You must meet any number of girls. What about all the nurses, or are you too lofty for them?'

'They are all so pretty and young and already spoken for,' said Simon lightly.

'When I phoned your secretary answered. Is she as pretty as her voice?' asked the younger of his sisters-in-law. She laughed. 'I didn't say who I was—at least, I said I was Mevrouw van Graaf. I thought you might not like her to know about your family... Hospitals are gossipy places, aren't they?'

The professor sat back in his chair and said placidly, 'She is even prettier than her voice. I hope you will all meet her some day, for I intend to marry her!' He looked down the table at his mother. 'You will like her, Mama.'

His mother smiled. She was a handsome woman whose dignified appearance concealed a gentle nature. 'If you love her, my dear, then I shall too. Will you bring her here to meet us all?'

'I hope to, but not just yet.' He smiled. 'I believe that she doesn't like me very much.'

There was a ripple of laughter. 'Simon, what do you mean? Why doesn't she like you? Have you been horrid to her?' This from his youngest sister.

'No, no. I have behaved with great correctness towards her. Somehow we started off on the wrong foot—and she has a sharp tongue.'

'Just what you need,' said Celeste. 'I'm going to like her very much. What is her name?'

'Julie—Julie Beckworth. She has green eyes and bronze hair, very long and thick, and she is what the English call a fine figure of a woman.'

'All curves?' asked Celeste.

'All curves,' agreed Simon.

Dinner over, they gathered in the drawing room on the other side of the wide hall. It was a splendid room, the polished wood floor covered with lovely rugs, their colours muted by age. The windows were tall and narrow, draped in old rose brocade, and the same colour covered the comfortable chairs scattered around. There were vast cabinets against the walls and a very beautiful long-case clock between the windows.

Arranged here and there there were lamp-tables, as well as a sofa-table behind the enormous sofa facing the stone fireplace. A fire was burning briskly and Jason, asleep before it, roused himself to go to his master, although an elderly labrador, his mother's dog, merely wagged her tail and went back to sleep.

'You'll be able to stay for a few days?' asked his mother. 'It was such a quick visit when you were last here.'

'Two days. I must go back to Leiden for a few days...'

'Does Julie know when you're going back?' asked Hugo.

'No. I'm not absolutely sure myself.'

Jan, who looked after the house with his wife Bep, brought in the coffee and they sat talking until late. It was midnight before they all dispersed to their rooms.

Simon, strolling round the garden in the chilly night while the dogs had a last run, wished very much that he had Julie with him. He wanted to show her his old home and he wanted her to meet his mother and his family, but he would have to be patient.

The dogs settled in the kitchen, he went up the oak staircase at the back of the hall and along the wide corridor to his room. As he passed his mother's door she opened it.

'Simon, dear, I'm so very happy for you. I was beginning to think that you would never find her—your ideal woman—but now that you have I shall welcome her with open arms.'

He bent to kiss her cheek. 'Father would have approved of her, my dear.'

He went back to Leiden two days later, to Siska, waiting for him with a splendid supper and anxious to hear the news from Huis Driesma. 'I hope I'll be seeing you again soon,' she observed. 'I'm that happy about the young lady—took to her at once, I did.'

The professor, hardly able to wait before he should see Julie again, nevertheless delayed his departure so that he might meet several of his friends and colleagues at the hospital. But three evenings later he drove down to the Hoek, boarded a ferry and sailed for England.

It was cold, misty and overcast when the ferry docked at Harwich. He drove up to London and let himself in to his cottage. Blossom might be getting on a bit, but his hearing was excellent—he was in the hall almost before the professor had shut the door.

'Welcome back, sir.' He uttered the words with grave pleasure. 'Breakfast or an early lunch? You probably fared indifferently on board the ferry.'

'Breakfast would be nice, Blossom.' The professor glanced at his watch. 'I'll miss lunch, but I'll dine here this evening. I'll have a shower while you cook.'

The temptation to go straight to St Bravo's and see Julie was very great, but first he must get his affairs in order. Having eaten a splendid breakfast, he got into his car and drove to his consulting rooms.

Mrs Cross, his receptionist, was there at her desk. 'Oh, good you're back,' she observed. 'I wasn't sure when you would be back—you didn't say.' She cast him a reproachful look. 'But I've booked several appointments for tomorrow, starting at four o'clock. I said I'd phone if you weren't back today.'

'Splendid, Mrs Cross. Anything in the post that I should know about?'

'Plenty. Can you spare the time now, or will you be in tomorrow morning?'

'I'll see to them now. If you bring your notebook I'll give you the answers and you can get them out of the way.'

The afternoon was well advanced by the time he had finished dictating. He drank a cup of tea with Mrs Cross and then drove to the hospital. The late afternoon traffic was building up and it took much longer than usual. Perhaps Julie would already have gone home...

It wasn't quite five o'clock as he opened his office door. She was kneeling on the floor, sorting a pile of papers into neat heaps. The overhead light shone on her hair, turning it to russet streaked with bronze, and he paused for a moment to relish the sight.

As he closed the door she turned her head, and he wished that her face wasn't in shadow. He had wanted to see how she looked when she saw him.

'I didn't expect you,' said Julie. 'I'm not nearly ready with all this.' She sounded cross, and he thought ruefully that it wasn't quite the greeting he had hoped for.

'Well, now I am here,' he said placidly, 'supposing I give you a hand?'

CHAPTER SEVEN

THE professor squatted down beside her but she didn't look up. His hands, large and well-shaped, sorting the papers, sent her insides fluttering with the sheer delight of seeing them—to look at him would have been fatal. Her own hands were shaking—something which he noticed at once with satisfaction, although he reminded himself ruefully that she might be shaking with rage at his sudden return.

He asked politely, 'You have been kept busy? Is Miss Frisby not yet back?'

Julie said in an indignant voice, 'Not for another two days...'

'You had difficulty coping with her work?' he asked gently.

'Difficulty? Difficulty?' Julie slapped a pile of papers with some force. She drew a deep breath. 'Her teeth must have been giving her a great deal of trouble.'

The professor suppressed a grin. 'You have reduced chaos to a tidy state?'

'Yes. Do I have to stay there until she returns, now you're back?'

'Certainly not. I shall probably erupt into a maelstrom of work which won't leave you a moment for anyone else. What are all these papers?'

'Referred notes from patients you have been asked to examine. Some of them are from other hospitals. I've classed them as far as possible.'

She got to her feet and he did the same, towering over her. 'Your post is on your desk, sir. I've dealt with the routine stuff and your private mail is on your blotter. You may wish to take it home with you.'

He glanced at his watch. 'Get your coat; I'll drive you home.'

'Thank you, but there is no need . . .'

'I don't think need comes into it. Get your coat, Miss Beckworth.'

'I have just said—' began Julie, and stopped when she caught his eye.

'Julie,' said the professor, in a voice which she didn't care to ignore. Besides, he had called her Julie. A slip of the tongue, or deliberately said to persuade her?

She fetched her coat, and when he opened the door went past him without looking at him. He must have had a splendid time in Holland, she reflected, and most certainly he must have seen the girl from Groningen. Perhaps the way now lay clear for them to marry. She closed her eyes for a second at the thought and tripped over the doormat.

The professor scooped her up neatly and stood her back on her feet. The temptation not to let her go was so fierce that he was compelled to release her briskly, an act which unfortunately she misinterpreted.

Her lovely face was a mask of haughtiness as she got into the car—something he chose to ignore, talking cheerfully of nothing in particular as he drove the short distance, and when she asked him in a quelling voice if he would like to come in, her stony face daring him to do so, he remarked that he would be delighted.

The warmth of Mrs Beckworth's and Esme's welcome more than made up for Julie's coldness. He was offered coffee and Luscombe produced an apple cake he had just taken from the oven.

'Glad ter be back 'ome?' he enquired chattily. 'Not but what you've an 'ome in foreign parts. Still, I dare say you've friends in London?'

'Us,' said Esme. 'We're friends, aren't we?'

'Of course you are,' declared the professor. 'And that reminds me—I have tickets for *La Bohème*—Saturday evening. I would be delighted if you would be my guests?'

Esme flung herself at him. 'Oh, yes—yes, please. Opera—and it's that marvellous singer.' She turned to her mother. 'Mother, say yes, do please . . .'

'That's very kind of you, Simon. It would be a wonderful treat.' Mrs Beckworth looked as delighted as Esme.

Julie didn't say anything at all.

'Shall we dress up?' asked Esme, filling an awkward pause.

'Er—well, something pretty . . .' The professor, so fluent when it came to unpronounceable medical terms, was at a loss.

'Will you be wearing a dinner jacket?' asked Mrs Beckworth. 'We none of us have anything very fashionable, I'm afraid.'

The professor looked at Julie. 'When I saw you at the Café Royale you were wearing something silky and green—that would be exactly right.'

'That old thing,' declared Esme. 'Julie's had it for years. It suits her, though.'

'That's most helpful, Simon,' said her mother. 'We wouldn't want to embarrass you.'

'I'm quite sure that would be impossible, Mrs Beckworth. May I fetch you shortly after seven o'clock?'

He went soon afterwards, bending to receive Esme's kiss, shaking hands with Mrs Beckworth and wishing Luscombe a friendly goodnight, but giving Julie no more than a casual nod, with the reminder that he would see her in the morning.

Esme was on the point of remarking upon this, but before she could utter her mother said, 'We must settle this clothes question. Esme, finish your homework; we'll talk over our supper. Yes, I'm sure Julie will help you with your essay while I talk to Luscombe...'

In the kitchen she sat down at the table where her old and devoted servant was making a salad. 'Toasted cheese,' he told her. ''Is nibs popping in like that didn't give me no time for anything else.'

'Well, yes, we weren't expecting him. It's very kind of him to invite us out. If you would like to have Saturday afternoon and evening off, Luscombe, we shan't be back till late. I think we'd better have a kind of high tea before we go, and we can get that for ourselves.'

'OK, Mrs Beckworth. There's a film I'd like ter see—I could go to the matinee and 'ave tea at my sister's.' He was cutting bread. ''Is nibs didn't so much as look at Miss Julie. 'E's smitten, all right, and so's she, bless 'er. 'E'd better love 'er dearly, or I'll wring 'is neck for 'im!'

Mrs Beckworth acknowledged this generous offer in the spirit with which it had been given. 'We would be lost without you, Luscombe. Ever since the doctor died you've been our faithful friend.'

'And 'appy to be so, Mrs Beckworth.' He put the bread under the grill. ''Is nibs is right for our Julie. All we need's a bit of patience while they discover it for themselves. At cross purposes, they are, aren't they?'

'Yes, Luscombe, I do believe you're right. We'll just have to wait and see.'

Over supper the important question as to what they should wear dominated the conversation. Julie, secretly surprised that the professor had noticed what she had been wearing, agreed that the green jersey would do. Her mother had what she called her 'good black', which was instantly vetoed as being too dull. 'There's that grey silk you had for your silver wedding,' she said thoughtfully. 'If I alter the neck there's that bit of lace in the trunk in the attic—I could turn it into a jabot.'

Esme was rather more of a problem. There were four days before Saturday, and nothing in Esme's cupboard which would suit the occasion.

'There's that sapphire-blue velvet cloak you had from Granny, Mother,' Julie said. 'There's enough material in it to make a pinafore dress for Esme. If you get a pattern I could cut it out tomorrow and run it up on the machine. You'll need a blouse, Esme— have I got anything? There's that white short-sleeved one of mine—I can take it in everywhere and add a blue bow at the neck. If it doesn't turn out we can rush out on Saturday afternoon and find something.'

The professor, pursuing his own plans, took care to be away from his desk as much as possible during the next few days. It meant that he had to work late after Julie had gone home, but it also meant that save for dictating his letters he needed to see little of her. True, she accompanied him on his ward-rounds, but so did half a dozen other people; there was no fear of being alone with her.

It wasn't until Julie was on the point of leaving on Friday that he said casually, 'I'll see you tomorrow evening—I did say shortly after seven, did I not?'

'Yes, Professor. We'll be ready,' Julie replied, and added, 'We're looking forward to it.'

She went home then, intent on finishing Esme's outfit—which had turned out surprisingly well. The blue suited her, and although they all knew it had originally been an old cloak no one else did, and the blouse, taken in drastically, was mostly concealed under the pinafore.

On Saturday evening, dressed and ready, they inspected each other carefully. Mrs Beckworth looked charming—the jabot had made all the difference and she was wearing her amethyst brooch. Esme preened herself in childish delight, and Julie, in the green dress, hoped that the professor wouldn't find them too unfashionable.

He arrived punctually, complimented them on their appearance, and helped Mrs Beckworth into the cashmere coat.

'We share the coat,' Esme told him chattily. 'It's Mother's but Julie wears it too, and just as soon as I'm big enough I shall be allowed to borrow it as well.'

Not a muscle of the professor's face moved; he ignored Mrs Beckworth's small distressed sound and Julie's sharp breath.

'You'll be a charming young lady in no time,' he observed. 'I like the blue thing you are wearing.'

'You'll never guess—' began Esme.

She was brought to a halt by Julie's urgent, 'Esme, no.' And Luscombe, coming into the hall to see them off, proved a welcome diversion...

Much later, lying in bed, too busy with her thoughts to sleep, Julie mulled over the evening. It had been wonderful; the Opera House had been magnificent, the audience sparkling and colourful, and the singing magnificent too—more than that, it had been breathtakingly dramatic. As the curtain had come down on the last act Julie had wanted to weep at the sadness. She hadn't been able to speak, only to shake her head and smile when the professor had asked her if she had enjoyed it.

He had driven them to the Savoy Grill Room and given them supper, and Esme, she remembered thankfully, had behaved beautifully—although her eyes had been sparkling with excitement and it had been obvious that she was longing to stare around her and make remarks. Her mother had said little, but Julie hadn't seen her look so happy for a long time.

She, herself, knew that there would never be another evening like it; it was something she would treasure for the rest of her life, something to remember when the professor became once more coldly impersonal and addressed her as Miss Beckworth.

She closed her eyes at last on the happy reflection that the blue velvet pinafore dress had been a great success; even though the seams and finish wouldn't bear close inspection, no one would have guessed...

*   *   *

The professor hadn't guessed but he had suspected—
a suspicion confirmed by Esme, that outspoken child,
who, finding herself alone with him for a few moments, had confided that it had been made out of her
granny's old evening cloak.

'It took Julie three days—she's ever so good at
cutting out and we've a very old machine, but it
doesn't work very well. It's best not to look inside
and inspect the stitches, but it's nice, isn't it?'

'It's charming,' he had assured her gently. 'And no
one would have any idea that it wasn't brand-new from
one of the best shops.'

A remark which had encouraged her to tell him
about her mother's lace jabot...

It was a relief that the next day was Sunday. It gave
Julie time to remind herself that just because the professor had invited them out to such a splendid evening
it didn't mean that he felt any friendlier towards her.
He was behaving very strangely too. She was never
quite sure of him—one minute coolly disinterested,
bent only on the work in hand, the next asking friendly
questions about her mother and Esme.

The professor, on the other hand, was well pleased
with the evening.

Late though it was by the time he had let himself
into his little house, Blossom had still been up.

'A pleasant evening, I trust, sir?' Under his severe
exterior Blossom hid a soft heart and a real fondness
for his master. 'Mrs Venton telephoned to remind you
that you are lunching at her house tomorrow. I am
to tell you that Professor Smythe and his wife will
be there.'

The professor, his head full of Julie and the way she had looked during the last act of *La Bohème*, had given an absent-minded nod. Even the mention of Professor Smythe, old friend and respected colleague though he was, had roused no interest in him just at that moment. Later, of course, when he had disciplined his thoughts to be sensible, he would look forward to seeing him again.

When they did meet the next day, over drinks at Audrey Venton's house, they were given little chance to talk.

Mrs Venton was a woman who liked to be the centre of interest. She was well aware that she was attractive, well dressed and an amusing companion, and she expected everyone else to think the same. She also expected to monopolise the conversation.

The professor, who had from time to time taken her out to dine, discovered that he no longer had any interest in her. Lunch was a lengthy meal, and when the Smythes got up to leave he made the excuse that he had to call in at the hospital and left with them.

'Perhaps we could have an evening out soon?' asked Audrey.

'I'm afraid not—there are the students' exams coming up. They'll keep me busy for some time—marking the papers.'

'I'll phone you . . .'

'A delightful lunch,' he told her smoothly, and remembered the Beckworths' kitchen, with a cake on the table and everyone drinking mugs of coffee. The conversation might not be scintillating but it was spontaneous and sometimes amusing, and everyone listened to everyone else . . .

Seeing Professor Smythe and his wife into their car outside, he put his head through the open window. 'Will you dine with me one evening soon? Just the three of us? We had no chance to talk.'

'We'd love that,' said Mary Smythe. 'I'll bring my book or my knitting and you two can discuss whatever it is you want to discuss. How do you get on with that dear creature, Julie, Simon?'

'She's a splendid worker...'

'Had you noticed that she was beautiful too?'

'Yes—she isn't easily ignored, is she?'

His elderly friend asked, 'How did she get on in Holland? Never got into a flap with me, but of course we never went across the channel.'

'Took it in her stride—worked like a beaver.'

'Good. Aren't you glad that I bequeathed her to you?'

'Indeed I am.' He smiled suddenly. 'You have no idea how glad!' He withdrew his head, saying, 'I'll give you a ring about dinner.'

He stood on the pavement and watched Professor Smythe drive away. He in his turn was watched by Audrey Venton from behind the drawing room curtains. She was clever enough to know that what little interest he had had in her had gone completely, and she wondered why.

As for the professor, he went back home, finished an article for a medical journal and then sat back to think about Julie. He was quite capable of making her fall in love with him, but he had no intention of doing that—love, if there was any love, would have to come naturally from her. All it required, he concluded, was monumental patience. Although, of course, if fate cared to intervene in some way, he would be grateful.

Fate did intervene.

The fire alarm sounded just after five o'clock on Monday, while Julie, requested by the professor to find the old notes of a long dead patient, was patiently going through the racks of dusty folders housed in a vast bare room just under the hospital roof. There were no windows—only a skylight, never opened—so she had to work by the aid of the strip lighting above the racks. There was another girl there too, one of the clerks attached to the records office, standing at the end of the room, close to the door. She gave a squawk of fright at the sound, dumped her papers and made for the door.

'Quick, there's a fire. We'll all be burnt alive.' The squawk became a scream. 'And all those stairs...'

'Only one flight,' said Julie. 'Probably it's only a small fire in the kitchens. You run on; I'm just coming.'

She kept her voice calm although her insides were quaking as she put back the folders she had taken from the rack—and at the same time she saw the folder the professor wanted. She tucked it under her arm and started towards the door.

It was slammed shut before she reached it. The girl, in her hurry, had forgotten to slip the lock. There was no key on the inside of the door, which was a solid affair, fitting snugly into the wall. Julie turned the handle in the vain hope that a miracle would happen, but it didn't. The door was shut and she was on the wrong side of it.

She wasted a few minutes shouting, even though she knew that no one was likely to hear her—nor would she be missed. The professor would expect her to make her way to the assembly point for the staff and there was no reason to suppose that the nursing staff would miss her.

'A pretty kettle of fish,' said Julie, and cheered herself with the thought that the girl who had fled so hastily would remember that she had slammed the door shut. The attic was too remote for her to hear much, but faintly she caught the sound of the fire engines and then, faint but ominous, a crackling sound.

Something had to be done, and she looked around her.

There was a small solid table and chair for the convenience of those checking the folders. She dragged the table under the skylight and climbed onto it. Even by stretching her arms above her head she couldn't reach it. She got down again and began to pile folders onto the table. When she had stacked a goodly pile she climbed up again, and this time she could reach the skylight. The iron catch had rusted off and it was jammed.

She got down again and carried the chair over to the table, balanced it on the piles of folders and climbed back on. The chair was light, she ought to be able to smash the skylight . . . She remembered the notes the professor had wanted, and got down again to fetch them. She climbed back as quickly as possible—the little puff of smoke finding its way through a minute crack in the door warned her to waste no time.

All the same, she paused for a moment—if smoke could get through cracks in the door maybe if she waited until it collapsed in the fire she could escape down the stairs... Second thoughts revealed the futility of such a scheme; she climbed carefully, dragging the chair after her and, since she was a practical girl, with the professor's folder tucked under one arm.

She raised the chair above her head, wobbling uncertainly on the pile of folders, but it was awkward lifting the chair and the prod she gave the skylight was no more than a tap. She lowered the chair, and at the same time the lights went out.

It was evening outside by now, and raining. She stared up into the dark outside, so frightened now that she couldn't think.

The sound of the skylight being opened almost sent her off balance.

'Hello,' said the professor from the dark above her, and shone a torch onto her upturned face, suddenly lightened by a glorious smile.

'Oh, Simon,' said Julie.

She couldn't see his face clearly, couldn't see his slow, wide smile. He said cheerfully, 'I see you've started to escape. Good. Now, this may be a bit tricky—I'm going to have to heave you out. The moment you can reach the edge of the skylight get a grip of it so that I can shift my hold a bit.'

She said idiotically, 'I've found those notes you wanted.' And went on, 'Couldn't you open the door, and then I could come through? I'm awfully heavy!'

'Too much smoke. I'm awfully heavy too; I dare say we'll manage very well between us. Only do exactly as I say.'

'Yes, I'm ready.'

'Lift your arms and don't whatever you do fall off the table. I shall probably hurt you; I rely on you not to burst into tears or have hysterics.'

Julie said crossly, 'What do you take me for?' and lifted her arms.

He began to haul her up, inch by inch. The iron grip on her arms was almost more than she could bear—if he were to drop her... She went stiff with fright.

'Relax,' said the professor calmly, and went on heaving, his powerful arms straining. It seemed like a very long time before he said, 'Now try and get hold of the sides and hold on very tightly. I'm going to move my hands.'

Julie let out a squeaky gasp and did as she had been told, and then she squeaked again as his hands slid from her arms and held her in a crushing grip.

'Now heave yourself up a bit. I've got you safe and I'm heaving too. You're almost out.'

It took a few more anxious minutes before she tumbled out in an untidy heap. 'Don't move,' said the professor, and flung a great arm across her. 'There's a slope here. We'll lie still for a moment and get our breath.'

Julie reflected that standing up would be difficult—moving of any kind would be impossible. She had no breath and she ached all over. She lay thankfully under the shelter of his arm and felt his heart thudding mightily against her.

Presently she gasped, 'Thank you very much—you saved my life. How did you know I was there?'

'Well, I asked you to come here, didn't I?' He gave a rumble of laughter. 'I can't afford to lose my secretary, can I?'

A remark which brought tears to her eyes. She gave a sniff and told herself that it was the kind of remark that she might have expected.

'Why are you crying?'

'I'm not...'

'It's a good thing it's dark—we must look a fine pair, spreadeagled on the tiles. Now, the next thing to do is to attract attention. There's a low parapet round the roof, and we have to slide down to it. Slowly, hanging on to everything handy as we go. Ready?'

He kept his arm around her and began to edge his way down. 'You won't fall; I have you safe.'

It was a tricky business, and hard on the knees and hands, but finally they reached the narrow gutter and felt the parapet against their feet.

'Keep perfectly still. I'm going to stand up.'

The professor rose to his splendid height, put two fingers in his mouth and whistled. He repeated the ear-piercing noise until he heard a shout from the ground below, and a moment later a searchlight almost blinded him.

He sat down then, content to wait until they were rescued, putting a hand on Julie's shoulder. 'Stay as you are,' he told her. 'We'll be home and dry in a very short time. Have you stopped crying?'

'Yes. I am sorry.'

He patted her shoulder. 'You have been a dear brave girl, Julie.' He gave a chuckle. 'We're wet, aren't we?'

She nodded in the dark. 'Is it a bad fire?'

'The medical wing.'

'That's under here.'

'Everyone has been got out.'

'Not us...'

'Very soon now. I'm quite happy here, aren't you?'

'Yes. I don't think I've ever felt so happy. What's that noise?'

'The fire brigade's ladder.'

A cheerful voice from the other side of the parapet accosted them.

'Getting a bit wet, are you? I'll have one at a time…'

'I'm not going without you,' said Julie.

'Yes, you are, and don't do anything on your own.'

'Young lady, is it?' The fireman shone his torch. 'Best to lift her in without turning her.'

Two pairs of hands shovelled her gently over the parapet and onto the ladder. She kept her eyes shut; if she opened them she would scream. 'Don't be long,' she mumbled to the professor, and was borne to the ground, feeling sick.

'Oops-a-daisy,' said the fireman cheerfully. 'We're on the ground, missy! I'll go back up for the gentleman.'

'He's a professor,' said Julie, and added, 'Thank you very much.'

She was whisked away then, trundled in a chair to Casualty, on the other side of the hospital, where she was clucked over by the dragon in charge, divested of her sodden clothes and cleaned up and plastered where plaster was needed.

'Lucky girl,' said the dragon, 'nothing serious—a few cuts and scratches. Was it Professor van der Driesma who got you out? A man of many parts. That silly girl, panicking and slamming the door—didn't tell a soul either. Only he went round looking for you and she plucked up courage to tell him. Silly with fright, poor girl.'

She took her phone from her pocket as it bleeped.
'She's fine, sir—a few bruises and cuts. Nothing a
good sleep won't cure.' She listened for a moment.
'I'll send her home now. A good hot bath and bed.'
She listened again and laughed, then turned back to
Julie. 'You're to go home. I'll parcel up your clothes
and you can go in that blanket. I'll get an ambulance.'

'He's all right—the professor?'

'Sounded normal enough to me. Giving a helping
hand, he said.' The dragon eyed her thoughtfully.
'Those bruises on your arms are going to be painful—
how did he get you out?'

'Through the skylight. He pulled me out.'

'Very resourceful. You're not exactly a wisp of a
girl, are you?'

'No. I told him I was heavy but he wouldn't listen...'

'Well, no, I don't imagine he would. Lie there while
I get that ambulance.'

Julie, swathed in a grey blanket, was driven home—
away from the chaos of the hospital. The fire was
under control now, but there was a good deal of smoke
and great pools of water.

'A nasty fire,' said the ambulance driver. 'Lucky
no one was hurt, though I dare say it shook up some
of the patients. As soon as they've been checked, we'll
be ferrying them over to New City and St Andrew's...'

He stopped the ambulance then, and her mother
came running out.

'Half a mo', love. I'll carry the young lady in—she
can't walk without her shoes.'

'Oh, yes, of course.' Mrs Beckworth opened the
door wide and Julie was carried into the sitting room
and laid on the sofa.

'A cup of tea?' her mother asked the driver. 'I know you can't stay, but there's one ready in the kitchen...'

'If it's made...'

Julie thanked him and sat up as Esme came racing downstairs. 'Whatever happened?' she wanted to know. 'Simon phoned and said you were being sent home for a rest. He said there's been a fire.' She eyed Julie. 'Why are you wearing a blanket?'

'I've no clothes. We had to lie on the roof, and it's raining.'

Mrs Beckworth came and sat down on the edge of the sofa. 'Esme, go to the kitchen and get a mug of tea for Julie. She'll tell us what's happened when she's rested.'

'I'll tell you now,' said Julie. 'I'm quite all right— only a bit scratched and bruised.' She took the mug Esme offered and Luscombe, ushering the driver out, followed her in.

'Gave us a fright, Miss Julie—and there's the phone...' He went to answer it. 'It's 'is nibs. Wants you, Mrs Beckworth,' he reported.

The professor's voice was almost placid. 'Julie's home? Good. She needs a warm bath and bed. I don't want her to come in tomorrow—let her have a lazy day.'

'Yes—yes, all right, Simon. You can't tell me what happened now—I expect you're very busy. She'll tell us presently.'

'She's a brave girl. I must go.'

He rang off, and Mrs Beckworth went back to sit by her daughter.

'That was Simon, dear. Just wanted to make sure you were safely home and to say you're not to go to work tomorrow.'

'He saved my life,' said Julie. 'He pulled me through a skylight. He must have hurt himself.'

'He sounded all right, love. Why a skylight?'

Julie finished her tea and Luscombe came back with a plate of thin bread and butter and the teapot. 'I'll explain,' she said.

It took some time but no one interrupted, and when, at length, she had finished, Luscombe said, "E's a bit of all right, isn't he? I'm going to put a hot water bottle in your bed, Miss Julie, and when you've had your bath I'll bring up a drop of hot milk and a spot of brandy.'

He went away and Mrs Beckworth said, 'Darling, you've had an awful time—thank heaven Simon found you. You could have been....' She choked on the word. 'We can never repay him.'

'I can think of all sorts of ways,' said Esme. 'I'll go and run a bath—and you'd better have Blotto with you tonight for company.'

So Julie, still wrapped in the blanket, went upstairs presently and got into a bath, and her mother exclaimed in horror at her bruised arms.

'They look worse than they are,' said Julie untruthfully. 'I expect he's bruised too.'

Tucked up in bed, drowsy with the brandy and milk, and with Blotto pressed close to her, Julie slept.

The professor, letting himself into his house at three o'clock in the morning, was met by Blossom. 'A fine time to come home, if I may say so, sir! I trust you've suffered no hurt and that the fire is now under control. I gather from your telephone call that no one was injured.'

He sounded disapproving, but he had a fire burning brightly in the study and a tray with coffee and sandwiches ready on the desk. He fetched the whisky and a glass and poured a generous measure.

The professor sat down tiredly. 'Thanks for staying up, Blossom. I'll go to bed presently. Everything's under control at the hospital. I'll go in as usual if you'll give me a call around eight o'clock. Goodnight.'

Blossom, dignified in his plaid dressing gown, went to the door. 'I must say that I am relieved that you are none the worse, sir. Goodnight!'

The professor drank his whisky, swallowed the coffee and sandwiches and stretched aching muscles, thinking of Julie. Safe in her bed, he hoped, and sleeping. Upon reflection he concluded that he had rather enjoyed himself on the roof. He hoped that the next time he had his arms around Julie it would be in a rather more appropriate situation.

Presently he went to his bed, his tired muscles eased by a long hot shower. When he woke later and went down to his breakfast there was nothing about his elegant appearance to suggest that he led other than a pleasant life and an uneventful one.

Julie woke late and Luscombe brought her breakfast in bed. 'Had a good sleep, Miss Julie? Your ma's on her way up and I'm off to the shops—chops for supper tonight, and I'll make a macaroni cheese for lunch.'

'You're an angel, Luscombe, but I feel fine. I'm going to get up presently.'

The bruises looked rather awful in the morning light, and the scratches and little cuts and grazes were sore, but they didn't seem to matter. Her mother sat on the side of the bed while she ate and Esme, on her

way to school, came to see how she was and gobble
up the last slice of toast. 'If Simon comes give him
my love,' she said airily, and clattered downstairs and
banged the front door.

'Of course he won't come,' said Julie to her mother.
'I'm going to get up.'

The secret wish that he would come she kept hidden;
he had no reason to do so. Tomorrow she would go
back to work and he would be the professor again,
not Simon, holding her fast on that awful roof.

'Now I'm home for the day,' she declared, 'I'll make
myself useful.' And when her mother protested, she
said, 'I'm going to polish the silver.'

'Your hands, darling...'

'I'll wear gloves.' She sat down at the dining room
table with the spoons and forks, and the small pieces
of silver that her mother treasured, and started work.

CHAPTER EIGHT

JULIE didn't hear the professor arrive; her mother had seen him drive up from the sitting room window and had opened the door to him before he could knock. It wasn't until Julie turned round, suddenly aware that she was being looked at, that she saw him standing in the doorway watching her.

'Hello, Julie,' said the professor, and crossed the room to take her hands in his and remove the rubber gloves she was wearing. He examined them in turn. 'Did they give you an ATS jab?' he asked.

'I think so, but I'm not quite sure. I was being sick...'

He pushed the spoons and forks to one side and sat down on the table.

'I'd like to take a look at your arms.'

Julie took off her cardigan and rolled up the sleeves of her blouse. The bruises were a vivid purple, blue and green, the marks of his fingers very clear. He examined them very gently, observing, 'They are going to hurt for a few days, I'm afraid. I'm sorry.'

'Yes, but you got me out—the bruises don't matter. Did—did it hurt you pulling me up? Your muscles must be so tired.'

'A little stiff.' He gave her a gentle smile and she was suddenly shy.

'I'll never be able to thank you enough...' she began, 'I—'

Her mother's voice from the door stopped her from saying something she might have regretted. 'There's coffee in the kitchen—you won't mind having it there, Simon?'

They sat around the kitchen table, the professor, her mother, Luscombe and Julie, drinking their coffee and eating the fairy cakes her mother had made, and the talk was cheerful and easy—and if Julie was rather silent, no one mentioned it.

Presently the professor got up to go. He shook Mrs Beckworth's hand, clapped Luscombe on the shoulder, told Julie that if she felt like it she could return to work in the morning and bent and kissed her cheek, leaving her with a very pink face. Her mother pretended not to notice and walked out to the car with him.

I mustn't interfere, reflected Mrs Beckworth, but spoke her thought out loud. 'Do you like Julie, Simon?'

He smiled down at her. 'Like her? I love her, Mrs Beckworth. I'm in love with her and I intend to marry her. I believe that she loves me, only there is something that won't allow her to show her feelings. I have no idea what it can be but I have plenty of patience— I'll wait until she is ready.'

'I didn't mean to ask,' said Mrs Beckworth. 'Interfering, you know. Only I'd said it before I could stop myself.'

'You will be a delightful mother-in-law,' said the professor, and got into his car. 'And you will like my mother.'

She watched him drive away and went back to the kitchen. Julie wasn't there.

'Gone back to that polishing,' said Luscombe. 'How's the lie of the land?'

'Just what you and I hope for, Luscombe. But all in good time.'

Her faithful old friend and servant nodded his head. 'That's OK, by me, ma'am—as long as the end's a happy one.'

'I'm quite sure it will be.'

The professor was deep in discussion with one of the medical consultants when Julie arrived back the next morning. He wished her good morning in an impersonal voice and resumed his talk and presently he went away, which gave her time to assume the mantle of the perfect secretary and sort out the post, find the right page in his diary and fetch the patients' notes he had listed.

It was mid-morning before she saw him again, when he returned to read through his post and dictate his letters. Not once did he mention the terrifying happenings on the roof. She went to her dinner eventually, where she was surrounded by eager acquaintances anxious to hear exactly what had happened.

'Weren't you terrified?' someone asked.

'Yes. I never want to feel like that again.'

'I bet you were glad to see Professor van der Driesma's face peering down at you.' The speaker was a pale-faced girl given to spiteful remarks. 'He must be as stout as an ox—you're no lightweight, Julie.'

A cheerful voice chimed in. 'I wouldn't mind being rescued by someone like the Prof. I don't suppose he swore once . . .'

'No, he didn't—anyway, it would have been a waste of breath, and he needed all he'd got. As Joyce said,

I'm no lightweight.' Julie studied the cottage pie on her plate. 'Just how much damage has been done? Does anyone know?'

'Well, it's not as bad as it might have been. The whole wing is gutted, but the rest of the place escaped damage. The secretaries have had to move across to the surgical side, somewhere in the basement, and a lot of equipment went up in smoke. It could be worse.'

When she got back to her office the professor was at his desk. 'I'm going over to the New City,' he told her. 'There are several patients bedded there that I must check. If I'm not back, go home as usual.' He glanced up at her, pushing his spectacles up his handsome nose. 'Arms all right?'

'Yes, thank you, sir. You have a consultation in Manchester tomorrow at two o'clock.'

'I'll be in to go through the post with you before I go. I should be back here some time in the evening.'

He turned back to his desk, once more immersed in his work, and she went to her desk and began to type the letters he had dictated.

If it hadn't been for the pain in her arms and the almost healed scratches, the night of the fire might have been a figment of her imagination. He had kissed her too—not that it had meant anything. Probably given in the same spirit as he would pat a dog or stroke a cat, and already forgotten. She shook her head angrily to dispel her thoughts, and applied herself to her typing.

The professor went presently, wishing her a bland good afternoon, and she was left to thump her machine with unnecessary vigour. She was finished by five o'clock and ready to go home, but she lingered briefly, tidying her desk and then his, careful not to move any of the papers. His diary was open still and she glanced at it and saw his scrawl at the bottom of the page: 'Phone Groningen'.

'And why not?' she asked herself out loud. 'It's a perfectly natural thing to wish to speak to the girl you're going to marry.'

Perhaps he would make a joke of his rescue of herself, make light of it.

Julie took herself off home and spent the evening helping Esme with her homework and cutting up the windfalls from the old apple tree in the garden, so that Luscombe could make apple jelly. He liked to do that for himself actually, but it was obvious to his fatherly eye that she needed to be occupied. She went to bed early, pleading a headache, and wept herself to sleep.

She greeted him coolly in the morning, made sure with her usual efficiency that he had everything he needed with him, and when he had gone settled down to clear her desk. She was on the point of going to her dinner when one of the junior registrars came in— a pleasant young man she had met on several occasions. He had some papers for the professor and handed them over and then lingered to talk.

'Going to the hospital dance with anyone?' he asked diffidently.

'No.' She smiled at him as she laid the papers on the professor's desk.

'Then would you go with me? I'm no great shakes as a dancer, but I dare say we could amble round the floor.'

Why not? thought Julie. I'll have to start all over again making a life for myself. 'Thank you. I'd like to go with you. It's a week tomorrow, isn't it? Shall I meet you here?'

'Would you? If I wait in the entrance hall for you—around half past eight?'

'Yes, that suits me very well. I may have to leave before the end—you wouldn't mind?'

'No, no of course not. I look forward to it. Probably won't see you again before the dance—but you'll be there?'

She assured him that she would. She hadn't gone the previous year because Esme had had the measles. She had no idea if the professor intended to go. 'Not that it is of the slightest concern to me,' said Julie aloud, and went away to eat her dinner.

She had nothing to wear and little more than a week in which to solve that problem. She and her mother, with occasional unhelpful advice from Esme, combed through their wardrobes and then the trunks in the attic. They laid out the results on her mother's bed, and from them contrived a suitable ensemble. A grey chiffon dress, so out of date that it was fashionable again, high-heeled sandals, which pinched a bit but were just right with the dress, and a little brocade jacket which concealed the rather out-of-date cut of the dress's bodice. With minor alterations it would do very well.

'And of course you can have the coat,' said Mrs Beckworth. 'Is he nice, this young man who is taking you?'

'One of the junior registrars—Oliver Mann.'

'Does Simon go to these dances?'

'I've no idea. I suppose he'll have to put in an appearance—to dance with consultants' wives and the senior staff.'

Mrs Beckworth, glancing at her daughter's face, refrained from asking more questions.

The professor appeared to be his usual rather aloof self, intent on his work and giving her more than enough to do, but on the evening before the dance, as Julie was getting ready to go home, he looked up from his desk.

'Are you going to the dance?' he asked.

'Yes.' She returned his stare. 'With Oliver Mann—he's a junior—'

'Yes, I know who he is.' His usual bland voice sounded harsh. 'I hope you have a very pleasant evening.'

She very much wanted to ask him if he would be there, but that might look as though she expected him to dance with her. She wished him goodnight and went home to try on the grey dress once more.

The hospital dance was an annual affair and everyone went—from the most junior of the student nurses to the hospital governors—if their circumstances permitted. Julie, dressed and wrapped in the coat, her stylish sandals already nipping her toes, got into the taxi her mother had insisted upon her having.

The entrance hall at St Bravo's was thronged, but Oliver was looking out for her, and once she had left her coat in the improvised cloakroom they made their way to the hospital lecture hall—a vast place, decorated now with streamers and balloons. The dancing had started some time ago and they joined the crowds on the dance floor.

Julie, looking around her, was thankful for the crush. Her dress, compared with most of those around her, wouldn't stand up to close scrutiny. Oliver didn't notice that, though. He told her awkwardly that she looked nice, and swung her into an old-fashioned foxtrot.

He had been quite right—he wasn't a good dancer. He had no sense of rhythm and every now and then he trod on her feet...

The music stopped and he said enthusiastically, 'That was great. I hope the next dance is a slow one— you know, the kind where you can stay in the one place all the time.'

And which would be a good deal kinder to her feet, reflected Julie.

The next dance was a waltz, an 'excuse-me', and they had circled the room once before someone tapped Oliver on the shoulder and she found herself looking at the vast expanse of the professor's white shirt front.

She glanced up briefly. 'I didn't think you'd be here.'

'Of course I'm here, so that I may dance dutifully with all the right ladies.'

So it was a duty dance! thought Julie peevishly. She might have known it. She said with a snap, 'Well, at least this duty dance doesn't have to last too long. Hopefully someone will come along and relieve you of one of them at least.'

'Tut-tut, you are too quick with your guesses.' He looked down at her and wondered with a flash of tenderness from where she had unearthed her dress. Not a made-over cloak, but definitely not *haute couture*.

Whatever it was, she looked beautiful in it—but then she would make a potato sack look elegant.

He ignored the tap on his shoulder from one of the radiographers and swung her into a corner of the room. 'You are enjoying yourself?'

'Very much. Oliver is rather nice, you know,' she improvised quickly. 'We've known each other for some time.'

'Indeed.' The professor, who didn't believe a word of that, sounded no more than polite, and she rushed on quickly.

'He's from Leeds, and hopes to get a job there when he's finished here. From what I hear, it's a rather nice city. I'm sure I should like it.'

The professor didn't allow himself a smile—not even a twitch of the lip. 'You wouldn't mind living so far away from your family?' he enquired politely.

What had she started? thought Julie, and plunged even deeper into deception. 'Oh, no! One can always drive to and fro,' she added airily.

'Indeed one can.' He was all affability. 'And when are we to be given the glad news—wedding bells and so on?'

If Oliver were to come now she would die. 'Oh, there's nothing definite.'

'I'm glad to hear that. I hope you will stay until I leave.'

'Leave? Leave? You're going back to Holland, of course.' She had gone quite pale.

'Not entirely—merely altering the balance of my work. I'll still have a consultant's post here, but I shall undertake much less work here and more in Holland.'

She said, unable to help herself, 'You're going to get married?'

'It's high time I did, isn't it?' He spoke lightly, and when one of the medical students tapped him on the shoulder he handed her over with nothing more than smiling thanks.

After that Julie danced and laughed and talked, and now and again caught a glimpse of the professor dancing with his colleagues' wives and then with the pretty theatre sister and the even prettier Outpatients sister.

She and Oliver shared a table with several others, but the delicacies laid out for their consumption were dust and ashes in her mouth. She danced again after supper, for she danced well and was in demand as a partner, but she longed for the evening to end.

It was after midnight when she saw her chance and told Oliver that she was leaving. When he protested, and then said that he would see her home, she told him lightly that a taxi would be waiting for her. 'It's been a lovely evening, Oliver, and thank you for inviting me. You go back and do your duty on the dance floor. There's that nice staff nurse from Casualty casting eyes at you...'

'You don't mind? I mean, I'll take you home with pleasure...'

'I'll be there in ten minutes, and I mustn't keep the cab waiting.' Out of the corner of her eye she had seen the professor looking at her from across the floor, which prompted her to kiss Oliver's cheek before she slipped away.

It took a few minutes to find her coat. The attendant—one of the servers from the canteen—was sleepy and impatient, but once it was found Julie nipped smartly towards the hospital doors. She didn't relish her solitary walk home and she hoped there might be a late bus or a real taxi, but she didn't care. Anything was better than staying there watching the professor smiling down at his partners . . .

It was dark, very dark, and the bright lights streaming from the hospital seemed to make it darker. She paused for a moment and put out a hand to push the doors open.

There was no mistaking the long-fingered elegant hand which came over her shoulder, gave her her hand back and opened the door.

'It isn't raining,' said the professor breezily. 'The car's close by.'

He bustled her across the courtyard and into the Bentley, and it was only when he had got in beside her that she found her breath.

'This is quite unnecessary, Professor,' said Julie coldly.

'My dear girl, you're behaving foolishly—trotting off home in the middle of the night in this neighbourhood. That's what you intended to do, wasn't it? What fairy tale did you spin to young Oliver?'

'I'm not a child—' began Julie.

'Something which I have discovered for myself. And for which I am thankful.'

Julie sat bubbling over with temper, at the same time aware of heartfelt relief. Only a fool would traipse the streets at that hour of the night, and only her disappointment over the evening had overridden her caution. She had been silly to feel disappointed too; there was no reason why the professor should even have nodded to her, let alone danced with her . . .

The professor had nothing to say either, and he had stopped outside her front door before she could decide whether to speak.

'Is there someone waiting up for you?' he wanted to know.

'No. I have a key. Thank you for bringing me. I hope I haven't spoilt your evening.'

He turned to look at her. 'The answer to that is so complicated that I'll say no more. Give me your key.'

She handed it over meekly; there were times when it was wise not to argue with him.

'Stay there while I unlock the door.' He got out, opened the door and switched on the hall light, came back and helped her out, then waited while she went indoors. She had to say something, thought Julie desperately.

She turned to face him. 'I'm sorry I've been silly. Thank you for bringing me home. Goodnight.'

She looked very beautiful, standing there with the dim light from the hall shining behind her. The professor resisted a strong urge to take her in his arms and kiss her, but he sensed that she was in no mood to be kissed. He bade her a cheerful goodnight, adding the rider that he would see her on Monday morning, and when she had gone inside, shut the door, got back into his car and returned to the hospital.

There was still an hour or more before the dance would end, and the more senior the member of the staff the more obligatory it was to remain until the very last note from the band.

The first person he saw when he entered the hall was Oliver, looking worried.

'Anything wrong?' asked the professor.

'No, sir—at least, I came here with Julie—you know, your secretary—and she told me she'd be leaving before the end and that she had a taxi coming for her.' His youthful brow furrowed. 'I should have made sure that it was there.'

'It was.' The professor, who only lied when it was absolutely necessary, considered that it was necessary now. 'Julie got in and was driven away. I wished her goodnight and she answered me.'

The relief in Oliver's face was very evident. He gave the professor a disarming smile. 'I say, sir, thanks awfully. I was a bit worried.'

The professor told him kindly to go and dance, and felt old. Too old for Julie? He had no chance to pursue the thought as the senior medical consultant's wife had tapped him on the arm.

'You should be dancing, Simon. You must know that half the nurses here are hoping you will do just that.'

'You're flattering me. I've a better idea...' He whirled her away while she laughingly protested.

Presently she said, 'Clive wants to talk to you— you'd better come to dinner one evening. I'm not supposed to know, of course, but you're thinking of making your headquarters in Leiden, aren't you? You'll still work here?'

'Oh, yes. But more or less on a part-time basis.'

'You have that charming little house here, though. Won't you miss it?'

'I shall be to and fro quite frequently—it will still be my home while I'm over here.'

'What a restless way to live, Simon. You ought to marry.'

'And live here permanently?'

She looked up at his face; its expression gave nothing away. 'No, I don't think you would do that.

I think your roots are in Holland, even though you choose to work here too.'

He smiled suddenly. 'Yes, they are. None the less, I hope to go on working at St Bravo's for a long time yet.'

'Oh, good.' The music stopped and they stood together on the edge of the dance floor. 'But I should like to see you married, Simon. Men need someone to look after them.'

'Don't let Blossom hear you say that!'

She laughed. 'He always looks so grumpy, but I think that secretly he would chop his right arm off for you.'

'Heaven forbid. But he looks after me splendidly when I'm over here.'

Simon danced until the band played a final encore, and then waited patiently with the senior hospital staff while the nurses and housemen said their goodnights and went off to their beds. There were a further five minutes or so while everyone agreed that the evening had been a success before they, too, went home.

The professor went quietly into his house, but not so quietly that Blossom didn't hear him—appearing silently on the narrow staircase, cosily clad in his dressing gown.

'Here's a fine time to come home,' he observed tartly. 'There's coffee on the Aga. Shall I fetch you a cup, sir?'

'I'll fetch it for myself, Blossom. Do go back to bed, there's a good fellow.'

Blossom turned on his heels, his duty done. 'Had a good time? Was that nice young lady there?'

'Miss Beckworth? Yes, she was.' The professor paused on his way to the kitchen. 'You liked her, Blossom?'

'Indeed I did. Danced with her, did you?'

'Yes.' For a moment the professor savoured his memories. 'Goodnight, Blossom.'

He went down to Henley in the morning, and wandered from room to room in his cottage there. Even in the winter it was pretty—small and old, and furnished with simple tables and chairs. His mother had come over to England when he had bought it and chosen curtains and covers, and Blossom had equipped the kitchen to suit his fancy. Simon wondered if Julie would like it as much as he did, with its pocket handkerchief of a garden bordering the Thames and the flowerbeds and the plum tree.

It was a haven of peace after his busy week at the hospital, and presently he went to the garden and began digging over the empty bed at its end, where Blossom had suggested that a herb garden might flourish. He worked for some time and then took himself off to the local pub for bread and cheese and beer and the friendly talk in the bar. He went back eventually, and finished his digging, then made himself a pot of tea and locked the little place up once more.

He would bring Julie to see it very soon, he reflected, driving back to London, and to make sure that she came he would invite her mother and Esme too.

Blossom had the day off, but he had left soup on the Aga and a cold supper ready in the dining room. And later, his meal over, the professor went to his

study and began to write an article for the *Lancet*.
He worked until he heard Blossom's key in the door
and then, after his loyal servant had gone to his bed,
he sat, his work forgotten, and thought of Julie.

Julie was thinking of him, her feelings mixed. She
was going to feel awkward on Monday morning and
she hoped that he would make no reference to her
stupid behaviour. She had told her mother that the
dance had been delightful, that she had danced every
dance, that the dress had been perfectly all right, and,
when pressed, had offered the information that the
professor had brought her home.

'You danced with him?' asked her mother, artfully
casual.

'Yes—once. There were an awful lot of people
there—you know, governors and their wives and
daughters. Some of their dresses were lovely.'

It was a red herring which her mother ignored. 'I
expect Simon looked very handsome...'

'Well, yes. I mean, men always look elegant in black
tie, don't they?'

'I hope he comes to see us soon,' chimed in Esme.
'I found a book in the library all about diabetes—
really gruesome—and I want to ask him about it. Do
you suppose he'll know?'

'I'd be very surprised if he doesn't,' said Julie. She
added carelessly, and with well hidden pain, 'He's
going to spend more time in Holland, by the way.
He'll still work at St Bravo's, but on a part-time basis.'

'He's going away?' Esme was upset. 'That means
I'll not see him again.'

'He's not going yet—at least, I don't think so. It's
just that instead of working part of the time in

Holland and most of the time here, he's changing it round.'

'I wonder why?' asked Mrs Beckworth.

Julie didn't answer.

She need not have worried about Monday. The professor was already at his desk when she got to work, glasses on his nose, his desk littered with patients' notes. His good morning was absent-minded and he didn't look up for more than a moment when he asked her to let him have the post as quickly as possible.

Whatever her feelings were, Julie knew her job; ten minutes later she laid the letters on his desk, sorted into important and trivial, and waited with her notebook and pencil while he read them. Presently he said, 'I'll leave you to see to these,' and handed back the pile of unimportant letters he had wasted little time over. 'I'll dictate these now.'

When he had finished—and how he managed never to be at a loss for a word in someone else's language always surprised her—he got up.

'I'm going to Birmingham. I should be back some time this evening. If I'm not in in the morning do whatever you think fit.'

He had gone while she was still telling him in a meek voice that she would do her best.

He wasn't there the next morning. She sorted the post, arranged his diary just so, made sure that his desk was exactly as he liked it and started on her own work. The phone never ceased to ring—various wards and departments wanted him and the path lab wanted him to phone the minute he returned. His registrar dealt with most of the queries she passed on to him, and when she asked him rather worriedly if the professor would be in that day, said in a non-commital voice that he supposed so.

She got on with her work—filling in various forms so that all he would have to do was sign them, making appointments, and all the while wondering where he was.

He was in her mother's kitchen, drinking the coffee Luscombe had made.

'I'm playing truant,' he explained, 'and I mustn't stay. But I wanted to ask you and Esme and Julie if you would like to come down to my cottage at Henley next Sunday. It's a pretty little place and delightfully quiet.'

'Oh, yes,' breathed Mrs Beckworth happily. 'We'd love to. Esme's dying to see you again—something about diabetes. It was diabetes, wasn't it, Luscombe?'

''S'right. Something to do with some islands, she said.'

'Ah, yes—they call some special cells the islets of Langerhans. I'm not an authority, I'm afraid, but I'll do my best to answer her.' He got up. 'I must go. Thank you for the coffee and I'll hope to see you on Sunday—about ten o'clock? Is that too early?'

'I'll see the ladies are ready,' Luscombe assured him, and went out to the car with him. 'A day out'll do Miss Julie good. A bit down in the dumps, she is.' Luscombe met the professor's eye. 'She's not happy, sir.'

'I know, Luscombe. But will you trust me to make her happy when the time's right?'

Luscombe grinned. 'That I will, sir.'

*   *   *

Back in his office, the professor contemplated the pleasing sight of Julie's downbent head, her colourful hair highlighted by the wintry sun edging its way through the small window of her office. He had wished her a brisk good morning and received an equally brisk reply, although she had gone a bit pink. She had bent over the computer again with a decided air of being busy, and he reflected that now was hardly the moment to invite her to join her mother and Esme on Sunday. Time enough for that; he was a man who could wait.

He waited until Friday afternoon, at the end of a tiresome day for Julie. She had finished finally, tidied her desk, made sure that everything was as it should be, and asked if there was anything else he wanted done.

'Thank you, no.'

She went to get her coat from the hook on the wall. 'I'll see you on Monday, sir.'

'Monday? Ah—it quite slipped my mind—we've had a busy week, haven't we?' He gave her a guileless look. 'Your mother and Esme are coming down to my cottage on Sunday. I hope you will come with them.'

She stared at him, her mouth open. 'Your cottage? Have you got another one? And Mother didn't mention it.'

'Oh, dear. Perhaps she thought that I would tell you. It seems that Esme has a great many questions to ask me... You will come?'

Her mother and Esme wouldn't go without her, and it would be unkind to deprive them of a pleasant outing. Besides, she wanted to see this cottage. She said reluctantly, 'Very well—since everything is arranged.'

'Splendid. I am sure you will like it—it is by the river at Henley. I'll call for you around ten o'clock.' He saw her hesitate, and added in a matter-of-fact voice, 'It's a place I shall miss when I go back to Holland.'

She thought fleetingly of the girl in Groningen, but he was going away wasn't he? He would forget them all once he was back in Holland, even if he came back from time to time. She had never given the girl cause to feel uneasy anyway...

She said soberly, 'I shall enjoy seeing your cottage, sir. Goodnight.'

That evening she asked her mother if she had forgotten to tell her about their outing. 'Professor van der Driesma didn't say a word to me; it was a surprise.'

'Oh, darling, how silly of me. I thought he would have said something to you and it quite slipped my mind—besides, I said nothing because I thought if Esme knew about it it might interfere with her schoolwork. She's so keen on all this medicine...'

Julie, her mind full of the prospect of a day with Simon, hardly listened to this excuse.

They were ready when he arrived on Sunday morning, warmly clad since it had turned cold and grey and threatened rain or even snow, and Blotto—securely attached to his lead and begged to be a good boy— uttered little yelps of pleasure, sensing that the day ahead would be something special.

Luscombe saw them into the car, exchanged the time of day with the professor and waved them off, before going back into the house to enjoy a quiet day on his own.

The professor had invited Mrs Beckworth to sit beside him, and Julie and Esme, with Blotto between them, were ushered into the back of the car. 'You shall sit beside me when we come home,' he promised Esme as he got in and drove off.

He crossed the city, the streets quite empty of traffic, joined the M4 at Chiswick and made short work of the journey to Maidenhead—taking a minor road for the last few miles to Henley-on-Thames.

The cottage, when they reached it, looked enchanting. It was near the bridge over the Thames, not far from where the Royal Regatta ended its course. It was a dull morning and very quiet. The professor parked the car and helped Mrs Beckworth out.

She stood for a moment, looking at the charming little place. 'It's perfect,' she told him. 'The kind of home one longs for.'

Esme had rushed through the gate to circle the cottage, peering in at the windows. 'Oh, Simon, may we go inside? Don't you wish you lived here all the time? You could, you know—drive up and down to the hospital each day...'

He opened the door and ushered them inside. 'Make yourselves at home while I fetch in the food. Does Blotto need a run?'

Esme went with him, and Julie and her mother stood in the tiny hall, looking around them and then at each other. 'He's already got that dear little mews house,' said Julie. 'And a house in Leiden...'

'I'm sure he deserves all of them,' said her mother. She pushed open a door. 'What's in here?'

CHAPTER NINE

JULIE and her mother were standing in the kitchen, admiring its perfection, when the professor and Esme came in—arms laden and Blotto prancing between them. They put everything on the kitchen table and he said, 'Shall we have coffee first, or a tour of inspection?'

'I'll make the coffee—I can always go round later,' said Julie. 'And shall I unpack whatever is in these boxes?'

'Will you? I left the food to Blossom. I hope there's enough . . .'

'For at least a dozen,' observed Julie, and opened the first box. Blossom prided himself on doing things properly; there was a Thermos of coffee, cream in a carton, the right kind of sugar and little biscuits. She arranged these on the table, found four mugs, then opened the other boxes.

Soup to be warmed up, and cold chicken, potato salad and a green salad, crisp and colourful, game chips and little balls of forcemeat. There were jellies in pots, thick cream, some chocolate mousse with orange, and caramel puddings packed separately, a selection of cheeses, pats of butter and an assortment of savoury biscuits. She stowed everything neatly into the fridge and peeped into the last box. Teacakes, more butter, tiny sandwiches, a fruit cake. Blossom was indeed a treasure.

172

The others came back presently, and they sat around the table while her mother and Esme exclaimed over the delights of the cottage. 'It's quite perfect,' declared Mrs Beckworth. 'How could you want to live anywhere else than here? It must be glorious in the summer.'

'Have you a boat?' asked Esme. 'Do you row?'

'Yes, there's a skiff moored at the bottom of the garden. We'll go and look at it presently, if you like.' He passed his mug for more coffee. 'But first Julie must see the cottage...'

He took her presently into the sitting room and stood while she wandered round looking at the pictures and picking up the delicate china and silver lying on the lamp-tables. 'Come upstairs,' he invited. 'But take a look at my study first. It's small, but ample for my needs.'

As indeed it was—furnished with a desk and a big chair, and with rows of books on shelves. It was deliciously warm from the central heating. As they went back into the hall Simon said, 'There's a minute cloakroom under the stairs.' He opened a little door to disclose it. It was small, but it had everything in it, as far as she could see, that was needed.

Upstairs there was a small square landing with four doors. The three bedrooms were furnished in pastel colours with white carpeting underfoot and Regency furniture, and the fourth door opened into the bathroom—surprisingly large and containing every comfort. It was a perfect little paradise and she said so.

'I can understand how much you must like coming here,' she told him as they went down the narrow stairs. For the moment she had forgotten her awkwardness with him, delighting in the little place, picturing him there on his own. Well, not for long, she reminded herself, and he watched her happy face cloud over and wondered why.

'Come and see the garden,' he suggested, and they all went outside and inspected the bare flowerbeds and admired the plum tree even though there wasn't a leaf on it.

'In the summer,' sighed Mrs Beckworth, 'I can just imagine everything growing—all those roses. Do you do the pruning yourself?'

They talked gardening for some time and then went indoors to set lunch on the table and warm the soup. The professor opened a little trap door in a corner of the kitchen and disappeared into his cellar to return with two bottles of Australian Chardonnay under one arm. They all had a glass while the soup was warming, and Julie popped the small crusty rolls into the oven to warm too.

She had been reluctant to come; there was no point in making her unhappiness and hurt worse than they already were, but now she forgot that for the moment. The wine was delicious, the little room was cosy, and just to be there with the professor sitting on the other side of the table was heaven.

As they ate and drank the talk was light-hearted with no awkward gaps—the professor, a seasoned host, saw to that. And presently, after they had drunk the delicious coffee Blossom had brewed in yet another Thermos, they tidied away the remains of their lunch and went for a walk beside the river, with Esme racing ahead with Blotto on his lead and Julie between her mother and Simon.

She hadn't much to say but the other two kept up a rambling conversation—the river, the pleasures of living away from London, the weather, the best places in which to take a holiday. She was astonished at the professor's capacity for small talk, and at how easy and friendly he was away from the hospital—easy with her mother and Esme, she reflected, but not with her. She was still Miss Beckworth, even if occasionally he addressed her as Julie.

They stayed out until dusk began to creep upon them, and then went back to tea—a leisurely meal, with Esme asking her endless questions and the professor good-naturedly answering them.

'When can I start training to be a doctor?' demanded Esme.

'If you work hard and get your A levels, when you are eighteen. It's hard work and goes on for years . . .'

'How long did you take to be a real doctor—I mean like a registrar?'

'Well, four years in Leiden, and then I came over to Cambridge and went to a teaching hospital in London—almost eight years.'

'You have Dutch degrees?' asked Mrs Beckworth. 'You must be awfully clever.'

'No, no. I'm lucky enough to have found the work I want to do and to have been given the opportunity to do it.'

In a little while they packed up, loaded everything into the boot and drove back to London.

The shabby streets around Julie's home were in cruel contrast to the cottage by the Thames, but Luscombe was waiting for them with a bright fire in the sitting room and the offer of coffee. The professor, when pressed to stay, refused.

'There is nothing I would enjoy more,' he assured
Mrs Beckworth, and stole a quick glance at Julie, 'but
I have an engagement this evening.' He took Mrs
Beckworth's hand. 'Thank you all for coming today.
It was most enjoyable.'

She smiled up at him. 'We've all had a lovely time—
thank you for asking us. We'll see you again before
you go off to Holland?'

'Yes, it will be some weeks yet. I've a good deal of
work to clear up here.'

He submitted to Esme's kiss, laid a gentle hand on
Julie's shoulder and went away.

'I don't want him to go,' said Esme. 'I wish he was
my brother or uncle or something.'

Julie silently agreed. Only she wished him to be
something other than that.

Monday was much as usual; there he was at his desk,
spectacles on his nose, writing furiously in a scrawl
she would be obliged to decipher presently.

His good morning was genial but he went back to
writing at once, leaving her to see to the post, answer
the phone and fill his appointments book. It wasn't
until the evening, as she was tidying her desk pre-
paratory to going home, that he looked up, through
the open door to where she was reaching for her coat.

'I'll drive you home,' he told her. 'It's a wretched
evening.'

She came to the doorway. 'There's absolutely no
need, thank you, Professor.'

'Need doesn't come into it. I should like to drive
you home.'

She twiddled the buttons on her coat. 'I'd much
rather not, if you don't mind.'

He stared across the room at her. 'I do mind. Do you dislike me so much? Julie?'

'Dislike you? Of course I don't dislike you.' She paused and then rushed on, 'It's because I like you that I don't want to come.'

'Oh, indeed?' He settled back in his chair. 'Could you explain that?'

'Yes, perhaps I'd better—and it doesn't matter because you're going away, aren't you? You see, I mustn't like you too much. It wouldn't be fair to her...'

'Her?' His voice was very soft.

'Yes—I saw you in Groningen, outside the hospital. I wasn't spying or anything, I just happened to be there...'

'Go on...'

'It was so evident that you loved—that you loved each other, and she's so pretty. I'm sure you love her dearly, but you're away from her for a lot of the time and sometimes you must feel tempted.' She looked down at her shoes. 'And—and...'

The professor, a man with iron self-control, allowed it to slip. He left his desk and folded her into his arms and kissed her. He had been wanting to kiss her for a long time now, and he made the most of his chances.

Julie didn't try to stop him; it was his bleep that did that. He let her go reluctantly and picked up the phone. He listened, then said, 'I'll come at once,' and strode to the door. 'Tomorrow,' he said, and gave her a smile to melt her bones.

She went home then, in a blissful dream which lasted until she got off the crowded bus and opened the door of her home, when good sense suddenly took over, leaving her dismayed and furiously angry with herself. How could she have been such a fool? To point out to him in that priggish way that he must feel tempted and then allow him to kiss her—perhaps he had taken it as an invitation on her part. Well, she would put that right—first thing in the morning.

She spent the evening rehearsing what she would say when she saw him, answering her mother's remarks at random and getting Esme's maths all wrong, and the next morning, after a wakeful night and no breakfast to speak of, she marched into his office full of good resolves.

The professor was telephoning, which was a drawback, and his good morning was exactly as usual—uttered in a voice devoid of expression. She went to her office, leaving the door open, took off her coat and arranged her desk, and the moment he had put down the phone and before she let her courage slide from her completely she went and stood in front of him.

'About yesterday,' she began. 'I should like to forget about it completely. That's if you don't mind.' He had looked up as she had spoken, and the expression on his face puzzled her. All the same, she went on, 'You'll be going soon, so it won't be...that is, there's no need for it to be awkward. I thought I'd like to clear the air before we—well, we might find it a bit awkward.' She added earnestly, 'You don't mind that I've said something about it?'

He looked at her over his spectacles. 'No, I don't mind, Julie. By all means forget it.' He sounded more remote than usual, and she supposed that she should be pleased about that. He looked at her, unsmiling, 'Let me have the post as soon as possible, will you?'

She spent the rest of the day worrying that perhaps she need not have said anything—he must think her a conceited creature to have imagined that a kiss was so important. Well, it had been for her. Her heart raced at the mere thought of it.

The day, like any other, wound to a close and she went home presently.

The professor went home too, to sit in his chair deep in thought.

'Your dinner is ready,' Blossom told him, faintly accusing. 'Didn't hear me the first time, I suppose. Got too much on your brain, sir.'

'I do have a problem, Blossom, but I'm happy to say that I've solved it. Something smells delicious.' As he seated himself at the table and Blossom ladled the soup he said, 'I may be going over to Holland very shortly. Just for a few days.'

'It'll be Christmas in a week or two.'

'Yes, yes. This isn't work. I'm going to Groningen to see my family. I shall be taking Miss Beckworth with me.'

Blossom allowed himself to smile. 'Well, now, that is a bit of good news, sir.'

'Let us rather say that I hope it will be good news.'

'A spirited young lady, if I may say so,' said Blossom, who, being an old and faithful servant said what he liked. 'Took to her at once, I did.'

'Which augurs well for the future.'

It seemed to Julie that during the next day the professor was very occupied. Moreover, the various departments and wards were constantly phoning him, and twice he had asked her to get a Dutch number for him and then, infuriatingly, had spent a long time speaking in Dutch to someone in Holland. Arranging to meet his future wife? she wondered. Discussing their wedding? Planning a holiday together?

Turning the knife in the wound hurt, but she couldn't help herself. She tried not to think of the months ahead without much success. They would be without him. If he intended to work at the hospital from time to time only then she wouldn't be needed by him; she would be transferred to another consultant and would probably never work for him again. Or see him. The quicker she got used to the idea the better!

The following morning when she arrived for work there was no sign of the professor. She saw to the post, arranged things to his liking on his desk and sat down in front of her computer. There was, thank heaven, a good deal of work to get through.

It was almost her dinner time when he walked into his office, and sat down at his desk. 'Anything urgent?' he wanted to know, and glanced through the letters she had arranged so neatly. 'No? Good. I shall be going to Holland in two days' time. I shall want you to go with me.'

He gave her a brief glance. 'There is nothing that can't be dealt with today and tomorrow. Will you ring my receptionist at the consulting rooms and ask her to deal with the appointments? She'll know what to do. Get hold of the path lab for me too, will you? I'll be on the ward if I'm wanted.'

He was at the door before she spoke. 'How long shall we be away, sir?'

'Three or four days—maybe less, certainly not more. There's too much to deal with at this end. We'll go as before, with the car.' He added gravely, 'You had better borrow the coat. It may be cold!'

Beyond that he had nothing further to say. She supposed that it was a seminar or a series of lectures, and she hoped that she would be staying with Mevrouw Schatt again. That was why he had made those telephone calls—to arrange to meet the girl. She went to her dinner and pushed beef casserole around the plate, joining in the chatter of the others with unusual animation.

Her mother took her news with a placid observation. 'That will be a nice change for you, dear. Sitting in an office all day must be so dull.'

Not when Simon's there, reflected Julie. 'Would you mind if I borrowed the coat? It might be cold.'

'Of course, love, and hadn't you better have some kind of a hat?' Mrs Beckworth pondered for a moment. 'There's that brown velvet that I had last winter—if you turned it back to front, with the brim turned up...'

They were both clever with their fingers, and the hat, brushed, pulled and poked into shape, sat very nicely on Julie's bright hair.

'Three or four days,' she observed. 'If I travel in a blouse and skirt and a thin sweater and take one dress that should do. Perhaps another blouse—and undies, of course.'

'You're not likely to go out?' asked her mother hopefully.

'No. When I'm not taking notes I have to get them typed up whenever I've time.'

It wasn't until the afternoon before they were to go that the professor told her that he would collect her at nine o'clock the next morning. 'We shall travel as before,' was all he said.

When he came for her, Julie, elegant in the cashmere coat and the made-over hat, bade her mother and Esme goodbye, assured Luscombe that she would take care and, after an exchange of civilities on the part of the professor; her mother, Esme and Luscombe, was ushered into the car.

Three, perhaps four days, she told herself. I must make the most of them. Only she hoped that she wouldn't see the girl again, and she must remember to be an efficient secretary and nothing more.

The journey was a repetition of the previous one: they boarded the Hovercraft at Dover, ate their sandwiches and drank coffee while the professor buried his commanding nose in his papers and once on shore wasted no time in small talk but drove steadily. They did not stop at the café they had eaten in before but crossed the Moerdijk Bridge and, after a mile or two, drew up before a restaurant, all plate glass windows with a row of flags waving in the wind.

'Off you go,' he told her. 'Over in that right-hand corner. I'll be here—I can spare half an hour.'

When she joined him there was a glass of sherry on the table, and he held a glass of tonic water in his hand. 'It will warm you up,' he said. He had stood up and then sat down opposite her again. '*Echte* soup,' he observed. 'Also very warming at this time of year. And an omelette to follow. I hope you don't mind me ordering, but we have quite a way to go still.'

That surprised her, for she had thought that Leiden wasn't all that distance.

'We're going to Leiden?' she asked. Really, it was time she was told a few details.

'Leiden? Briefly, to collect Jason. We're going to Groningen.'

She should have expected that. She supped her soup, drank her sherry and made short work of the omelette, then told him that she was ready when he was.

He was driving fast now, his hands light on the wheel, his face, when she peeped at it, placid. They were slowing through Leiden before she realised that they were there, and he drew up before his house.

'You would like to go indoors?' he asked, opening her door.

She nodded thankfully, wondering when the journey would end—Groningen seemed a long way off. He opened his door and Jason came bounding to meet them followed by Siska, who beckoned Julie to go upstairs and then turned her attention to the professor. They were still talking when she came down again, but the housekeeper shook her hand and smiled and opened the door. No time was to be lost, it seemed.

Julie longed for a cup of tea; it would make things seem more normal. She had the feeling that the day wasn't going as she expected.

With Jason breathing great happy gusts from the back seat they set off again. It had been a clear cold day, and now, although it was almost dark, there was a multitude of stars and half a moon creeping up the horizon.

Julie, lapped in warmth and the pleasant smell of good leather mingled with dog, decided sensibly to wait and see what was to happen. The professor had little to say and had offered no further information— presumably he took it for granted that she expected to go to the hospital.

He was travelling fast again, never recklessly, but overtaking everything on the road. Presently he asked, 'You are warm enough?'

'Yes, thank you.'

'I don't intend to stop again now we are back on the motorway.'

He didn't say much after that, and she made no effort at conversation. He was probably conning over a lecture, or thinking about the girl, and Julie had her own thoughts.

She was surprised when they flashed past a sign to Groningen—ten kilometres away. The time had passed quickly, and even as she thought it she saw the lights of the city ahead of them, clear in the flat landscape. Then he turned away from the motorway, along a narrow country road leading away into the dark fields around them.

'Is this a short cut?'

'It is the way to my home.'

'But you live in Leiden and London. Aren't we to go to the hospital?'

'No.' He drove on steadily, and Julie sat trying to think of something sensible to say. If they weren't going to the hospital but to his home—another home—why was that?

'I think you should explain.'

'Certainly, but not just yet.'

There were lights ahead of them and a very small village, and presently he drove through its short street and back into the empty country again. But not for long. Soon he turned the car between great gateposts and stopped before his home.

Julie sat where she was. The glimpse she had had of the house had rather taken her breath. It looked like an ancestral home and, sensible girl though she was, she wasn't sure what to expect now. The professor opened her door and helped her out, and let Jason out as well, and the three of them mounted the steps to the great front door. It was thrown open as they reached it and the girl standing there flung herself at the professor. He gave her a hug and disentangled himself.

'Julie, this is my sister Celeste,' he said. It was the girl Julie had seen in Groningen.

Julie went pale and then pink and took Celeste's hand, but her eyes were on his. 'Why didn't you tell me?' she asked.

'If you remember, I was interrupted.' He smiled. 'And in the morning you expressed a wish not to say anything more about it.' He turned to his sister. 'Are we all here?'

'Yes.' She switched to Dutch. 'She's gorgeous, Simon, we're all thrilled to bits. Have you quarrelled?'

'No. No. But I think for this evening we will remain sociable and nothing more. So no awkward questions, *lieveling*.'

'Ah, here is Bep to take your coat, Julie.' He saw her look. 'No, don't ask questions now. Let us have a pleasant dinner—I am sure you must be tired. Tomorrow is time enough...'

'For what?' She had the feeling that she was in a dream; she said so. 'It's like a dream.'

'Dreams come true, Julie.' And that was all he would say.

Hours later, lying snug in bed, convinced that she would never sleep, Julie tried to sort her muddled thoughts.

She had been swept into an enormous room full of people—well, not full, but five could be a crowd when you weren't expecting them—and they had welcomed her with smiling warmth just as if they had known about her. She had been given sherry and had presently crossed the hall to a dining room with dark-panelled walls and a table decked with white damask and a great deal of silver and crystal. She had sat next to Simon and eaten a delicious meal and taken part in a conversation not one word of which she could remember. Simon had had little to say to her, but he had been there, close by.

She had been taken to her room later by Celeste—a charming room, with a four-poster bed and dainty Regency furniture—and kissed goodnight and told to sleep well. Simon, she remembered sleepily, had opened the door for them and had smiled down at her in a way which had made her heart lurch...

She slept then, and didn't wake until a cheerful girl came in with a little tray of tea. There was a note folded between the teapot and the milk jug. The professor's familiar scrawl invited her to get up and come downstairs.

He was waiting for her in the hall, sitting in an enormous chair with Jason beside him. He got up and crossed to where she was hesitating on the last stair and took her hand. He led her to the back of the hall and opened a door there.

'Haven't you guessed, Julie?' he asked her. He turned her round to face him and put his hands on her shoulders.

'Perhaps just a little, but not until last night. I was afraid to.' She studied his tie. 'Why have we come here? I mean, I can see that you wanted me to meet Celeste—did you think I wouldn't believe you?'

'No. No, my darling. But you were cross, were you not? It didn't seem quite the right moment, and I wanted you here in my home, away from the hospital.'

'Oh, well—I'm here now,' said Julie, and looked up at him. She smiled and his hands let go of her shoulders, and she was caught close in his arms.

'I thought you didn't like me,' she muttered into his jacket. 'As a person, that is; I tried to be a very good secretary, because I hoped that if I was you'd notice me.'

'Dear heart, I have never stopped noticing you since the first moment I saw you. I shall continue to notice you until the end of time. I shall love you too, just as I love you now. Could we marry soon, do you suppose? We have wasted so much time.'

He kissed her then, and really there was no need to answer, but presently she asked, 'Your family— Mother . . . ?'

'My family know all about you, my love, and I phoned your mother last night.'

'Were you so sure?'

'Yes. And now be quiet, my dearest love, for I'm going to kiss you again.'

Julie smiled and didn't say a word!

Take 2 bestselling love stories FREE
Plus get a FREE surprise gift!

Special Limited-Time Offer

Mail to Harlequin Reader Service®

3010 Walden Avenue
P.O. Box 1867
Buffalo, N.Y. 14240-1867

YES! Please send me 2 free Harlequin Romance® novels and my free surprise gift. Then send me 6 brand-new novels every month, which I will receive months before they appear in bookstores. Bill me at the low price of $2.90 each plus 25¢ delivery and applicable sales tax if any*. That's the complete price, and a saving of over 10% off the cover prices—quite a bargain! I understand that accepting the books and gift places me under no obligation ever to buy any books. I can always return a shipment and cancel at any time. Even if I never buy another book from Harlequin, the 2 free books and the surprise gift are mine to keep forever.

116 HEN CH66

Name	(PLEASE PRINT)	
Address	Apt. No.	
City	State	Zip

This offer is limited to one order per household and not valid to present Harlequin Romance® subscribers. *Terms and prices are subject to change without notice. Sales tax applicable in N.Y.

UROM-98 ©1990 Harlequin Enterprises Limited

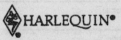

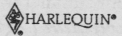

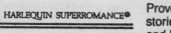

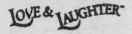

$\mathcal{H}$arlequin $\mathcal{R}$omance®

Coming Next Month

#3515 THE DIAMOND DAD Lucy Gordon
Garth had promised his wife diamonds for their tenth anniversary—
Faye didn't want diamonds, she wanted a divorce! But with two gorgeous
children and his beautiful wife at stake, Garth was determined to do all
he could to save his family!

The Big Event! *One special occasion—that changes your life forever.*

#3516 HEAVENLY HUSBAND Carolyn Greene
It seemed incredible, but when Kim's ex-fiancé Jerry woke from his
accident he seemed like a totally different man. Instead of a womanizing
workaholic, he'd become the perfect hero. He said she was in danger,
and that she needed his protection. But the only danger Kim could
foresee was that maybe heaven *was* missing an angel—and they'd want
him back!

Guardian Angels: *Falling in love sometimes needs a little help from
above!*

#3517 THE TROUBLE WITH TRENT! Jessica Steele
When Trent de Havilland waltzed into Alethea's life, she was already
wanting to leave home. So Trent's idea that she move in with him could
have been the ideal solution. But Alethea's trouble with Trent wasn't so
much that she was living with him, but that she was falling in love with
him!

Look out also for another great Whirlwind Weddings title:

#3518 THE MILLION-DOLLAR MARRIAGE Eva Rutland
Tony Costello only found out about his bride's fortune after their
whirlwind romance had ended in a trip to the altar. He couldn't forgive
her for being rich and for keeping it a secret. Melody had deliberately
tried to conceal her true worth for the sake of Tony's pride; now she
would have to fight to save their marriage. Rich or poor, she loved
Tony—she was just going to have to prove it!

Whirlwind Weddings: *who says you can't hurry love?*